PRA

THE ART (

Shortlisted, CBCA 2019

Shortlisted, Ethel Turner P
for the 2019 NSW Premier's Literary Awards

'Kernot's writing is imbued with life and grace
and moments of infectious joy.'
SA Weekend

'An exquisite lyrical verse novel…[a] sharply evocative tale.'
West Weekend Magazine

'Couples the swift, clipped charm of a verse novel and the
unpredictable beauty of the Australian landscape in a captivating
manner that showcases an author entirely comfortable with
her form…Lingers in the mind for weeks afterwards.'
Tulpa Magazine

'Kernot has created an intriguing tale of
mystery and the imagination with a haunting ambience
that the ghost of Edgar Allan Poe would recognise and
admire…This is a delightful story about grief transformed
and the urge to resurrect and to re-create.'
Saturday Paper

'This book is beautifully written…while the novel is
about grief, it is also about the importance of remembering
and keeping the memory of loved ones alive.'
Magpies Magazine

'An exquisitely crafted verse novel.'
NZ Listener Best Kids' Books of 2018

Sharon Kernot's first novel, *Underground Road*, was published in 2013; she has also published poetry and short stories. Her second novel, *The Art of Taxidermy*, was shortlisted for the 2017 Text Prize. Sharon lives in Mount Barker in South Australia with her family.

sharonkernot.com.au

THE
ART
OF
TAXIDERMY

SHARON KERNOT

TEXT PUBLISHING MELBOURNE AUSTRALIA

textpublishing.com.au

The Text Publishing Company
Swann House
22 William Street
Melbourne Victoria 3000
Australia

First published in Australia by The Text Publishing Company, 2018.
Reprinted 2019 (twice).

Book design by Imogen Stubbs.
Cover and internal illustrations by Edith Rewa.
Typeset by Text.

Printed and bound in Australia by Griffin Press, part of Ovato, an accredited ISO/NZS 14001:2004 Environmental Management System printer.

ISBN: 9781925603743 (paperback)
ISBN: 9781925626728 (ebook)

A catalogue record for this book is available from the National Library of Australia.

For Matt and Jess

LOVE

At the age of eleven
I fell in love
with death.
I found a gecko
in a dark corner
of a room.
Its lifeless eyes open,
its small bulbous toes
splayed
as if about to leap away.

I wanted to keep it,
to hold on.
I wanted to preserve
its lively expression.
I placed it on my dresser
and watched
its stomach deflate,
its scaly skin dry and curl
and the almost-leap
slowly decay.

SLEEPING BEAUTY

Later, I found a crow,
its feathers so black
they shone
with a blue tinge
in the bright sunshine.

It lay on its side
at the base of a jacaranda—
purple flowers scattered beneath—
as if it had fallen asleep,
floated down serenely
from a branch above.

I stroked its sleek feathers
expecting it to wake,
flap strong wings and fly off,
but it slept on.

I returned later
with a shoebox—
a cardboard coffin—
and carried my sleeping beauty
home to accompany my
withering gecko.

THE COLLECTION

Three brown tree frogs,
two skinks,
one New Holland honeyeater,
one ant-eaten galah,
one dusty sparrow
and one fresh, cat-killed
red-belly black—
perfect,
except for
four small puncture marks.

A GLASS HOUSE

Father bought
a large glass aquarium
to house them,
to contain
the fusty fug of death.

BURIED TREASURE

I discovered a sheep's skull
half-buried in a paddock
not far from the house.

I might never have noticed it
but for a small murder
of crows, feasting.

As I got closer, I could smell
the rotting flesh
and hear the hum of blowflies.

The crows *yarked*
and flapped away.
Blowflies scattered and buzzed.

The exposed side was picked clean
in places by birds and foxes.
White bone glinted in the bright day.

I tucked my nose and mouth
under my jumper
to avoid gagging

and sliced through a small piece
of woolly skin and sinew
until the skull came away.

The semi-buried side was damp with
skin and patchy grey wool,
and a withered eye.

ANNIE I

Annie was my best friend.
She was everything
I was not.

Her hair was the colour
of wheat at sunset,
her eyes as blue as a summer sky,
her lips the satin sheen of pink pearls,
her bone-white skin
never tanned.

She was pale and luminous,
a ghostly angel, but,
like me, she had a dark heart.

EGYPT

At school, Mr Morris
showed us slides of mummies,
long-dead kings and queens.

The earliest Egyptians
buried their dead in small pits
in the desert, where the heat
and dryness of the sand
dehydrated and preserved the bodies.

I thought of my sheep's skull
and its semi-buried side.

I borrowed books about the Egyptians
and found photographs
of ancient people
enduring beyond death.

Decomposition akin to art:
the shrivelled limbs,
the shrunken shoulders and chest,
the exposed clavicle,
the long ropey necks,
the perfectly preserved ear,
the missing nose,
the full head of hair crowning
the withered face.

I tore my favourite pages
from the books.

PRESERVATION I

I studied my beautiful corpses,
in their different states
of decay.

I preserved their scales and bones
and beaks and claws and feathers,
stroke by fastidious pencil stroke,

in dozens of sketchbooks,
with drawings and notes.

AUNT HILDA

That girl, she exclaimed,
having seen my latest addition—
the sheep's skull.
She is turning into a freak!

Annie and I peered through the crack
in the double sliding-doors.
Father smoked his cigar,
his full-bearded face expressionless.

She's fine.
His words, accompanied
by a large plume of white smoke,
drifted to the ceiling.

She is a girl, Wolfgang!
My aunt stood abruptly, hands on wide hips.
Charlotte needs dolls and…women.
Not dead things!

Father released a smoky sigh.
I knew what he was thinking—
It was not his fault that Mother had died
and we were left alone.

I will take her. She can live with me.

I held my breath. I could not bear it.

She is fine, Father said,
locking eyes.

I breathed out.

She has a scientist's heart.
It is in the genes. She is curious
and she is bright.

AUNT HILDA & UNCLE GRAHAM

Aunt Hilda lived in a cottage
around the corner and up the road—
turn left, then right, then left again.

Aunt Hilda had no children,
and Uncle Graham—
whose photographs
lined the mantelpiece
and an assortment of dressers
and hall tables and cabinets
throughout the house—
died in the war.

Uncle Graham's face radiated
cheerfulness,
Aunt Hilda's, contentment,
a modest, happy smile.
In every photo of them together
their arms or hands
or fingers were entwined,
their bodies turned slightly
towards each other.

I did not go to my aunt's house often
as she was mostly at ours,
cleaning and cooking and caring for me,
while Father worked
long days at the university.

But when I did go
I found the photos mesmerising.
I looked at them again and again
searching for clues of the past,
clues from the days
when my mother and father
were together,
happy.

MUSEUM

On a class trip to the dimly lit
Egyptian Room,
I could not tear my eyes away
from a pair of severed,
high-arched feet.

The bones almost visible
beneath the yellowed skin,
long and thin.

Talus, calcaneus, metatarsals, phalanges
hallux—long toes, third, fourth and fifth toes.
Mr Morris tapped the glass to the beat of
the names.

Those feet, the way
the mummified toes
curled claw-like—
especially the long, long toe—
looked just like Father's.

In the same cabinet
were two blackened hands,
one long and slender,
one small and thickly knuckled,
wearing a silver ring,

and a sleeping head
resting on a pillow.

A long straight nose
and a grimacing mouth
divided his face,
his eyelids half-closed over
dark holes.
Yellow light bounced from
his smooth black forehead.

He lay as lifeless
as a dark stone sculpture,
as indecipherable as
an Egyptian hieroglyph,
but thousands of years ago
he walked and talked
and breathed.

MOTHER'S ROOM I

I visited Mother's room.
Circled her silent bed,
ran my fingers along the edge,
tried to imagine her lying there
on her back.
Drifting into sleep,
not death.

Sometimes I climbed
onto the gold brocade bedspread
and lay with my arms
folded across my chest
like a mummy
or a coffin-bound corpse.

I never cried.
I do not remember much
about Mother.
She was a shadow
that hovered in the dark corners
of the house.

Her name was always spoken
in a whisper—
Adrianna, Adrianna.
Long vowels
rolling in waves
of pain through air.

WINTER I

Through my bedroom window
Annie and I watched
the grey day brighten
as the sun broke the clouds.

We breathed our own clouds
of condensation onto the cold glass
and watched yellowing leaves
drift down from the moulting robinia.

A wattle bird wrestled
with a moth on a branch,
its red cheeks lit like rubies
by the sudden sunshine.

We decided to go for a walk
to search for 'specimens'.
Father suggested this word,
for use around Aunt Hilda.

EXPLORATION

We marched along with a hessian bag
to the edge of the suburbs,
then weaved our way to the creek.

We walked with eyes cast down
scanning for specimens,
for any form of death,

but the day was teeming with life—
magpies speared the ground,
mudlarks picked through long grass,

galahs *chink-chinked* as they flew overhead,
rosellas chattered from distant bushes,
blackbirds scratched and foraged.

The ground was soft with mud,
winter grass and broad-leafed weeds
and little crops of fungi breaking through.

We walked and walked in the brittle air,
noses red and damp with cold,
fingers numb, shoes and socks wet.

The day brightened and darkened
as the sun swung through the afternoon
and then began to set.

Black clouds blurred the horizon
like dark mountains.
Others stained pink as the day died.

A GIFT

We headed home across paddocks
where white-winged birds
fought for roosts in the trees—
a clatter and cackle of corellas.

Annie grinned and took off
at breakneck down the hill
and the pack exploded into flight
and an ear-splitting chorus.

They wheeled overhead
and settled on the ground.
Annie galloped at them,
whooping with joy.

Again, the explosion
and a cacophonous cry, as they circled
and settled like white flags
in the surrounding gums.

And, like a gift,
one fell from the treetop—
landed with a dull thud at the base,
clambered and staggered.

We sat and waited.
Bagged our specimen, and carried it
through the cold, dark streets, back
to the fretful house to meet with trouble.

HOME

The house reverberated
with the clatter of silver, as Aunt Hilda
set the table, set the cutlery
down sharp.

We have been beside ourselves,
Charlotte. Sick with worry.
She pointed a fork at me
across the table.

Father frowned,
glared beneath bushy eyebrows.
Your aunt is right, Lottie. You must
be home before dark, before night.

We were about to call the police.
Your father could not stop pacing.
My heart is still aching from
the racing and the pounding.

I sat and listened, dutifully
nodded and stared down.
But the shining plates and glinting silver
were bursting with anticipation.

CORELLA

I unwrapped my dead bird,
placed it on my desk,
flicked on the lamp.

The feathers,
luminous,
as white as the frosty lawn
on a bright winter morning.

I stroked the velvety body
studied the details:
the strong feet and sharp claws,
the blue-grey ring around the eye,

the long curve of the beak
and the bright pink patch beside it.
The stretch of its wings
made me sigh.

The unfolding of bones,
the flight feathers like fingers,
the sulphur yellow underside
and tail feathers to match.

I wanted it to wake, to perch
on my shoulder, to cry its screechy cry.
Annie, I whispered, *Annie...*
Did we make it die?

FATHER'S STUDY

Father was on an outing
and the house was darkening.
It was mid-afternoon and already
the street lamps were glowing.

The fireplace blazed and crackled
in the lounge, throwing
out long, grey shadows
that made me think of Mother.

In Father's study I sat in his leather chair,
took a cigar from the wooden box,
leaned back, ran it beneath my nose
to smell his smell.

I put on his glasses, round and bottle-thick,
and the world blurred.
I stroked my imaginary beard
and sucked on the unlit Havana.

Outside, rain pelted the window,
the colours of the garden bled together
like an impressionist painting,
like Monet's garden.

I removed and folded his glasses,
reached for the magnifier
he kept in the ceramic pot with his pens,
the letter opener and an ornamental knife.

I struck a match and lit the cigar,
inhaled and coughed,
wandered around the room
with my magnifier, looking for clues.

I flicked on the reading lamp
and, illuminated in the window
reflected as darkly as my mother,
I saw my ghostly self:

long black hair,
pale-skinned and dark-eyed,
her pointy chin,
her blood-red lips.

I turned away, turned back for clues,
inhaled three short puffs
and coughed out
bitter smoke.

On a bookshelf, in a silver frame,
a black-and-white photograph
of Father (blond) and Mother (dark)
both straight-backed, unsmiling.

In a nearby wooden frame,
there is Father, Uncle Bernard and Opa
with three Japanese men, all smiling,
holding up leafy vegetables.

I returned to the desk, tapped
a roll of ash into the glass ashtray,
then opened the old tobacco tin,
fished out the hidden key,

and opened the drawer full of secrets.
Papers and passports and old photos
and the cool square lines
of Opa's Luger pistol.

SCHOOL I

For my science project
I took my corella to school.

Packed him into a small box,
cushioned on a soft, clean towel.

At the front of the classroom
I lifted him out, held him up.

Ew. Yuk. Gross.
Has it got maggots?

Does it smell? I bet it stinks.
How long's it been dead?
How did it die?

Be quiet class! Mr Morris said.

I told them where I found
my specimen.

I recited memorised facts.

The little corella is also called:
little cockatoo,
short-billed corella,
bare-eyed cockatoo,
blue-eyed cockatoo,
blood-stained cockatoo.

Corellas feed on fruits, grains,
seeds of grass and bulbs;
sometimes small insects.

They nest in tree hollows
lined with wood shavings.

They are social.
They live in large flocks.

The girls wrinkled their noses.
Some boys wanted to throw him around.

A new kid in the class
stroked the soft, white feathers.

He was as dark
as the corella was light.
His skin was rich like earth,
his eyes, oily brown,
his eyelashes, long and thick.

He wore knee-high, white socks,
black school shoes, polished—no scuffs.
His grey shorts and light-blue school shirt
were crisply ironed—with neat creases
down the length of each sleeve.

His long slender fingers
stroked the bird.
He's a beauty, he said.

Where did you come from? I asked.

From a mission. Long way.

He was the most beautiful boy
I had ever seen.
His quiet grace
and the stone stillness of him
reminded me of the Egyptian room.

WINTER II

When the robinia
turned skeletal and
exposed the wattle bird's
woody nest,
Annie and I went back
to visit the corellas.

The day was grey clouds.
Frozen rain
and blustery winds
whipped our hair
and bit our faces.

Dry, claw-shaped leaves
chased us
as we scurried away from the house.
A willy wagtail flitted
and sashayed
on the path ahead.

There were always birds.
But the lizards and snakes
were sleeping.
The ants had built high towers
around their nests, and
people were inside by their fires.

Puddles reflected miniature scenes—
the dappled sky, branches of trees,

the flight of birds, distant hills.
Annie splashed in them,
star-jumped and leapt.
Dressed in a yellow raincoat and boots,
she was like sunshine.

BIRDS

The corellas were grazing
with a scatter of galahs.
We sat on a fallen log
and watched them squabble and tussle,
beat their wings and waddle
like hook-nosed old men
with their arms tucked
behind their backs.

In the west, a distant rainbow
and shafts of sunshine
brightened the sky,
but not far away the clouds
were black and thick.

A prong of lightning flashed
and a roll of thunder
exploded the flock as if
a bomb had been dropped.

Annie gasped and smiled
with square white teeth.
Quick! she grabbed my hand
tugged me up
and we galloped away.

We ran across the paddock into
a thicket of trees and stopped
to listen to warbling birdsong.
I searched the treetop,
and looking back were
the red-brown eyes of magpies.

Look! Annie pointed to
a large untidy nest in the tree.
I wonder if it has any eggs,
she said as she climbed.
I followed—stretched and tugged,
heaved and hauled
myself behind.

There were no eggs,
but from that high-up branch
I could see all around.
Smoke rose from the chimney
of a distant house where a car pulled up.
A dark boy climbed out and
strolled to the door in the rain.

HEAT

At home, in the steaming air
and the sound of gushing water, I peeled off
wet jeans and socks,

lugged my sodden jumper over the tangled
snakes of my hair, then wrote
'Annie & Lottie' on the foggy mirror.

When I was naked, about to dip my toe
into the scalding bath,
Annie appeared beneath the water.

Her eyes were closed, her hands clasped.
Her hair floated and danced
around her face like yellow seaweed.

I plunged my foot in and she disappeared.
I took her pose—eyes closed, hands clasped—
and sank into the hot, hot water.

It stung my skin. My ears filled with silence.
My hair floated, tickled my nose, and I tried
to imagine what it would be like to die.

BETRAYAL

When I entered my room,
my hair twisted in a towel,
I smelt something wrong,
something too clean,
too sweet.

I flicked the light and saw
the emptiness.
The nothingness.
My beautiful creatures
were gone.

I ran to the lounge. *Father!*
He was in his favourite chair,
reading the paper,
smoking a cigar,
his calm legs crossed.

They are in the shed, Lottie.
He looked at me
over reading glasses.
Your aunt moved them.
They are fine.

Aunt Hilda emerged
from the kitchen:
Charlotte. They smell.
It is unhygienic, unhealthy.
We will have the authorities out.

No, we won't. No one cares.
That is not fair.

Your father and I discussed it.
We agreed it is for the best.
Your best.

I looked at Father.
He did not disagree.
He nodded solemnly and said,
Lottie, think of the shed
as your laboratory.

SCHOOL II

I sat next to Jeffrey
in the lunch shed.
He nodded, said nothing,

continued to chew
white triangular sandwiches
filled with cheese and
something green
like gherkin or cucumber.

His lunchbox sat open on his lap,
the lid tucked beneath.
Inside, neatly stowed, was an apple,
a lollipop, a slice of fruitcake.

My lunch was a mandarin
and a Vegemite sandwich on rough-cut bread
wrapped in brown paper.

We sat silently, side by side,
swung our long thin legs
back and forth, back and forth:

black and white,
black and white.

SCHOOL HOLIDAYS I

Aunt Hilda insisted
I sit in the lounge by the fire
and learn to knit.

We started with a scarf.
Knit one row, pearl one row.
Back and forth.

There was some solace
in that mindless act,
in the warmth of the fire.

Aunt Hilda was pleased
with my efforts: happy that I
had performed a girlish act.

Eventually, I escaped
to the shed, to my lab,
to visit the dead.

Father had put up shelves
and cleared a space
for my specimens.

It was not unlike his own lab,
with its chair and desk,
oil heater and bright lamp.

BLACK GOLD

Annie and I went to stay
at Oma's house
in the country, by the sea.

One morning
I woke in the thin light
to the sound of wailing.

I pulled back the curtains.
Circling over the small dam
were large black birds.

Annie! I called.
She rubbed her sleepy eyes
and joined me at the window.

I pulled on gumboots,
wrapped myself in a thick, dark coat
and hurried outside

to stand beneath the whirling birds
bigger than crows.
Cockatoos!

Long, graceful wings,
flight feathers like
splayed fingers.

They floated through the air.
Yellow-cheeked,
yellow-tailed.

Not at all like the corellas.
Elegant,
with a slow, deep wing-beat.

They wailed their eerie wail—
Wee-ahh, wee-ah, wee-ahh
and more birds came.

Like giant bats
they landed
in the eucalypts.

Annie and I crept,
working our way to them.

But with a clap of wings
and a mournful cry,
they fled.

OMENS

In the kitchen
Annie and I dabbed
paintbrushes at pictures
in a paint-by-numbers book.

It was a simple scene:
a small house on a hill,
with a plume of smoke billowing
from the chimney.

Oma was at the sink,
humming and slicing
onions and cabbage
for dinner.

Her gun-grey hair,
wound in a tight bun.
Her face as wrinkled
as the corpse of an apple.

Holz für das Feuer,
she said over bird-like shoulders.
Wood. Before supper.

We pulled on our coats
and our boots
and headed to the woodpile.
A blustery wind
blew us along the path.

The air was thick with sea salt.
I could taste it on my lips
as we gathered chunks of wood
and made our way back.

Clouds of pink coral
drifted above us,
almost close enough
to touch.

And then we heard the wailing
and stopped
and scanned,
and there they were.
Black-and-yellow cockatoos.

They flew overhead.
The yellow panels
of their tail feathers
looked to be painted on
with a thick square brush.

When Oma called
Abendessen! Lottie! Dinner!
we ran back to the cottage,
put the wood in the basket near the fire
and sat down for our meal.

All through dinner
the birds circled,
crying their sorrowful cry.
I could not see them
through the window
I could see only
the dappled sky.

Oma. The birds,
the black cockatoos,
I said and looked up
to where they might be.

Oma peered at me
through small clouded eyes
and shook her head.
Funeral birds.
Bad. Bad omen.

But they're beautiful.
She did not answer.
She chewed her cabbage
and meat, and the deep lines
of her mouth puckered.

OMA AND OPA AND OMENS

As we travelled homewards
I scattered the long silence,
asked why black cockatoos
are a bad omen.

Father continued to drive
looking ahead at the grey road.
His brow creased when he said,
It is because of the war.

I watched the lump in his throat
rise and fall,
and rise and fall again
as he swallowed.

*Black cockatoos swirled
like an ominous cloud
around the farm one year—
around the time that Opa died.*

*He died unexpectedly
during the war.*

*And now when Oma sees
a flock of black cockatoos
she thinks something terrible
will transpire.*

But Father, they are so beautiful
and graceful, and
they don't screech like corellas
or sulphur-crested cockatoos.

Father smiled. *You are right.*
They are beautiful and graceful
like black kites.
It is nothing, just superstition.

FUNERAL BIRDS I

I researched Oma's cockatoos:
the yellow-tailed black cockatoo,
also called yellow-eared cockatoo
and *psittacus funerous*.

Psittacus for parrot.
Funerous for their sombre plumage,
as if they're dressed for a funeral.

John Gould called them
Funeral Cockatoos
like the name Oma used.

Some Aboriginal people
call them *Wylah*.

Wy-la, Wy-la, Wyyy-laaaa,
the words floated through
my mind,
and I pictured
those beautiful birds
floating darkly
in the sky, crying
their mournful cry.

VISITING

On a bright winter's day
I found my way to
Jeffrey's house.

The sky was Wedgwood blue
and the clouds like
white figures on a china bowl.

The sun threw long shadows
on the road, from
naked street trees.

The yellow heads of soursobs
bobbed and swayed
in the gentle breeze.

At Jeffrey's door, I knocked,
and a grey-haired woman
answered, tipped her head to one side.

Yes? May I help you?
Her words were rounded,
clear and resonant.

Is Jeffrey home? I croaked
like a cockatoo.
There was a slight hesitation

before she opened the door,
showed me to the lounge,
asked me to *please, sit.*

The room was full of china figurines—
horses and dogs and deer and
ladies in beautiful dresses.

Ornately framed paintings
of English landscapes
hung on every wall.

Jeffrey stood stiffly in the doorway
like a dark ornament,
dressed neatly

in pressed shorts
and long socks, as if
about to go to church.

I asked him to come for a walk
to see the corellas,
but he shook his head, said:

I see them every day.
They fly round and round,
calling, screeching, crying.

A DANCE

I watched a documentary
about Aboriginal people.
The painted men danced, morphed
into kangaroos and emus.

The music—clapping sticks
and didgeridoos—
vibrated and resonated.

I saw a boy like Jeffrey—
a slow smile,
white, white teeth,
dark skin and hair,
gentle eyes.

The narrator explained
Aboriginal culture
in the rounded vowels
of the Queen.

That night, I dreamed
I was running, hiding from the drone
of a didgeridoo
as an old man
pointed a sharpened bone

and a flock of corellas
swirled in the sky
calling Jeffrey's name.

FATHER

Father took me to work
when Aunt Hilda
had a doctor's appointment.

His office was lined
with books, piles of papers
and filing cabinets.

He swivelled in his chair
and read with raised eyebrows,
while I drew pictures
sitting on the other side of his desk.

When a student knocked
softly on his door
I left them to talk, and I walked
the long campus corridors,
imagined I was a mouse or a rat
escaping the lab,
tunnelling my way out.

I went into the high-ceilinged library
with its ornate pillars and
rows and rows of reading tables
and shelves of hard-backed books.

Its coolness,
its hushed tones,
were like a church,
where everyone whispered
as they do at a funeral.

LUNCH WITH FATHER

We walked to the museum
to the Egyptian room,
where I stood in the gloom—
the half light—
and stared at the head
the feet, the hands.

They had not moved.
Nothing had changed.
Even the tingle that stirred
in the pit of my stomach
was the same.

I remembered the names
of the bones
Mr Morris had uttered:
Talus, calcaneus,
metatarsals, phalanges,
hallux.

I stared
with a longing
I did not understand.
Then Father
touched my shoulder,
led me
to another display.

DEATH POINTERS

As we threaded our way out
of the museum
I glimpsed photos
of dark-skinned people.

Not in white socks
or polished shoes.

Women and children
scantily dressed,
hair long and free.
Men with spears and shields,
wearing feathers and white paint.

Like the people
in the documentary.

In a glass case were two
long sharp bones labelled
'death pointers'.

The yellow bones were joined
by a twisted band of hair
glued with plant resin.

I was careful not to
line myself up with the point
of the bones, but
Father did not seem to mind.

I tugged at his arm and said,
Father, please move. The bones,
the death pointers,
are pointing at you!

He studied the bones for some time
and said, *Do not worry, Lottie,*
I'll be fine. It is only superstition,
like Oma's cockatoos.

TAXIDERMY I

On the way to the exit
I saw dead animals,
large and small—
climbing, crawling,
standing, rearing.

Father! Look!
They are perfect—
perfectly dead.
Not shrinking?
Not disintegrating?

There was no pungent smell,
just the soft wheaty scent of pelt.

They are preserved.
They have been stuffed
by a taxidermist.

Taxidermist?
I tried this new word,
rolled it around in my mind
and my mouth.

Father's voice shifted
into lecture mode
as he steered me back
to the campus:

Taxidermy is the art
of skinning and preserving,
then stuffing and mounting
the skins of animals…

TAXIDERMY DREAMS

All afternoon I tried
to recreate
the taxidermy animals.

While Father wrote,
I drew the beautiful,
dead creatures

from memory,
and longed to return
to study them again.

That night in bed,
in the haze between
wakefulness and sleep,

I revived them all.
Imagined them coming to life
with the magic of taxidermy,

which didn't just preserve—
but brought them back
from the dead.

MOTHER'S ROOM II

Annie and I crept into
Mother's room.
It had been closed,
and the air was chilled
and so still that I felt as if
we had entered a tomb.

I opened the wardrobe,
ran my hands along
her jackets and skirts,
coats and cardigans,
dresses and shirts.

I rubbed the woollen coat
I had seen in the photographs
along my cheek.
I inhaled Mother's smell—
a floral perfume
like the one on her dresser.

I powdered my nose,
rouged my cheeks,
painted my lips dark red.
When I twirled
in the long woollen coat,
Annie gasped—*You are Mother!*

I stared at the reflection
in the mirror,
tried to decipher
what the dusty image
was trying to tell me
about myself,
about my mother.

I looked into the eyes
that were hers,
that were mine,
but could not see
what was behind.

FOX I

We opened a drawer,
unleashing the scent of lavender
uncovering silky lingerie,
sheer stockings,
pointy satin bras.

Another drawer
contained gloves and scarves
and something animal
wrapped in tissue paper.
A skinned fox.

I lifted it out of its resting place,
stroked its reddish fur,
its little snout, its stiff ears.
Its mouth was clamped on its tail.
Its eyes were closed.

I put the sleeping stole—
the beautiful fox—over my head.
It tickled my neck,
hugged my shoulders, and
warmed my heart.

DEATH AT THE FUNERAL

We arrived darkly,
dressed in many layers.
I clutched the bundle
hiding under my coat.

Oma wept and moaned,
waddled and groaned.
Like a black cockatoo
in her cloak.

Aunt Hilda hovered over Oma,
clutching her bird-thin shoulders,
nodding and muttering,
dabbing a hanky at her red eyes.

Annie and I stood at the door
of St Mark's, where my eyes traced
the spire high into the sky, until
I was hustled inside—

into the chilly air,
where we slow-stepped
towards the open casket
at the front of the church.

Aunt Hilda grabbed my arm
sat me down on a pew
in the front row. Muttered, *Death
is not for children.*

I pulled Mother's stole
from beneath my coat
placed it around my neck,
then rejoined the queue
at the coffin.

Annie and I stared down
into the strange face
of death—
the face
of Uncle Bernard,
Father's twin.

We held hands
and stared and stared
at the dead body,
at the familiar face,
until Aunt Hilda roughly
bustled me back to my seat.

Her reddened eyes widened
at the sight of the sleeping
fox around my neck.

UNCLE BERNARD

All through the service
I thought of the face
of Uncle Bernard.

It was stone still
like the mummies,
but it was my uncle.

It was my uncle
but it wasn't. It looked
like him, but it didn't.

I knew he was dead,
but I did not feel it.

I hovered over
my feelings. And they
hovered over me.

It was hard to feel sad.
It was hard to feel
anything, except confusion.

I didn't understand.
I liked my uncle and
knew I would miss him,

but this was not real.
The man in the coffin
did not resemble my uncle.

The essence of him
had gone. His spirit had gone,
and in his place
a prostrate lifeless statue lay.

CLINGING

When you are a child,
when you are small,
you are almost invisible.

I do not think you understand.
It is not healthy.
Wolfgang, it is not normal.

Annie and I sat next to Oma,
who clung to
a procession of mourners.

Annie's hair shone
like a bright sun, like a star
amid the dark clothes.

The fox, the stole!
She is stealing through rooms—
that room.

Aunt Hilda was holding a plate
of sandwiches,
hissing into Father's ear.

Father scratched his beard
with his thumb and glanced at me.
Leave it with me, Hilda.

It is time to let go, Wolfgang.
Clear it all out. Why hold on?
Let it go. Let her go.

I stroked the furry hide
hugging my neck and
wondered what they meant.

MOTHER MEMORY I

There is the frantic scurrying.
The calling, the yelling.
The white skin whiter.
Lottie, Charlotte.
Come. Come now. Come. Now!
My arm being stretched,
as I try to keep up.
My legs not managing,
falling, stumbling.
Being picked up, roughly
swung onto a hip.
Crashing against bone.
Clinging to Mother's neck,
her dark hair knitted
between my fingers.
And then tumbling, both of us.
Heavily onto the soft earth.
The smell of grass.
The smell of cow manure.
The grey dam.
The grey, grey dam.
A shout echoing,
reverberating.
Stay! Sit! Stay there!
Fierce eyes, dark circles, faded lips.
The sound of splashing water.

SPRING

The days warmed and brightened,
but Father's mood darkened.

He stood at the window and
stared out at the garden,

his hands in his pockets,
his mouth clamped shut.

His papers and books were left
unopened, his dinner untouched.

Eat, Wolfgang. You need to eat.
Aunt Hilda hovered, clutching her apron.

I am sad, too. Her voice softened
and faltered, sounded

unlike Aunt Hilda,
more like Oma.

She dabbed at a tear
that trickled down her cheek.

We all miss our dear Bernard.
We miss him very much, but…

Her brow knitted together.
You have to think of Lottie.

Her hands opened in despair,
but Father did not respond.

Later that night she said:
It is hard for him, Lottie.

They were very close.
It is like that for twins.

He has lost yet another
part of himself.

WANDERING

The next day, Annie and I wandered
the streets in search of specimens,
leaving Father to stare at his window.

The sky was full of cottony clods
and, in the distance,
a small, black cloud loomed.

We passed cherry and
almond blossoms, and acacias
heavy with yellow wattle.

A bottlebrush was loaded
with crimson flowers
and two rainbow lorikeets

hooked upside down
like colourful chrysalises
stripping the tree.

We skipped along the road,
happy to be outdoors where
Annie's hair sparkled and glittered.

At the edge of the suburbs
where the paddocks began to spread
there were no corellas.

They've gone, Annie said.
*I thought they would stay forever
and ever. But they too have left.*

We followed a dirt track,
our ears listening to the birdsong,
hoping for a raucous corella call.

FLIGHTLESS BIRDS

Look! Annie pointed
at a small bird on the ground—
a baby magpie, lying on its back.

I inspected the bald head
twisted to one side
the long slender beak and bulbous eyes.

It was ugly and beautiful.
We looked up into the tree
and there was the nest.

We climbed up and up, until
a rush of air, a flap of wing and something
sharp struck my head.

I slipped down the trunk,
clung with one arm to a branch.
Lost my grip and dropped.

Then Annie yelped and tumbled
like a flightless bird,
landing on the ground with a thump.

We dusted ourselves off,
bagged our perfect baby
and limped home.

BRUISES

There were bruises
from the fall
on my shins and knees,
and scratches
from the rough bark.

Father did not notice
my limp or the cuts
surrounded by blue
or the shadows
under my eyes.

The baby bird slept soundlessly
in a shoebox—
a too-big coffin—
on a bed of woolly cotton.

I examined its flesh,
the patchy down of feathers—
black, white and grey—
the tiny under-formed wings,

the long sinewy neck,
the way its beak remained ajar,
the downward turn of mouth
radiating sadness.

FOX II

I wore the stole at school,
snuck it out of the house,
carried it in my bag until I was out
of Aunt Hilda and Father's sight,
then slipped it over my head.

The sleeping fox
warmed me,
absorbed the sense of dread
that had descended.

It was nice to have Mother close.
I felt her arms
draped around me.

The kids in the class said:
You're weird.
You're disgusting!
It's a dead fox.
You stink!

Jeffrey said:
Red fox. He's sly.
And he stroked
the soft fur hide.

A NOTE

Aunt Hilda waved an envelope.
You must not take that fox to school.
It is not right. It is not!

I didn't answer.
I ate my dinner quietly,
eyes downcast,

my fork making swirling patterns
in the thick, brown gravy
on my plate.

Later, Aunt Hilda spoke
to Father, who was drinking port
and staring out the window.

Wolfgang! You need to
snap out of this ennui…
this Verzweiflung.

I have a note from her school.
She wore that stole—the fox!—to class.
You must do something!

It is not normal, Wolfgang.
She is strange.
You must do something.

I slipped out to my laboratory,
and hid my lovely fox at the bottom
of a large cardboard box.

NON-VERBAL READING

The next morning
as Father folded his newspaper
his gaze caught my eye
and held it.

I waited for him to talk,
but he studied me through half-closed eyes
like I was a specimen
in his laboratory.

And then he nodded
and smiled his close-lipped smile, and asked,
How is school, Lottie?

It is fine, I replied.

He considered me further,
took mental notes with the same furrowed brow
he wore when he read or wrote.
Good, he said. *That is good.*

What are you reading? he asked
of the library book in front of me.

It's about Egypt. It's about tombs.

Interesting. He paused. *Is it interesting?*

Yes. Yes, it is.

And how are you?

I wondered what he meant.
I am good. I am well.

He scrutinised me a little more,
gathering non-verbal evidence perhaps,
before he finally said, *I am glad.*
That is good news.
We do not need to worry.

He opened his newspaper
and went back to reading.

JEFFREY II

Jeffrey walked home
from school with me
one warm afternoon.

We went the long way,
skirted the suburbs,
crossed the paddocks.

Jeffrey talked softly
sometimes,
but mostly not at all.

He lifted rocks and logs
and we watched worms wriggle
and ants and slaters scatter.

Where are the corellas?
I asked when we walked
in their empty territory.

Jeffrey shrugged. *They move.*
They fly away.
Why stay?

He caught a small skink,
opened his hand to show
the cool, flecked skin.

He stroked the sleek back,
smiled his slow smile.
Then let it go.

FRIENDS

At home, the kitchen was warm
with oven heat
and the smell of apple strudel.

Jeffrey sat at the table.
I poured us milk
and raided the cake tin.

When Aunt Hilda bustled in
she stopped and stared,
fiddled with her apron strings.

This is Jeffrey, Aunt Hilda.
He's come to look at my specimens.
Jeffrey rose from his chair and nodded.

Hello, Jeffrey. Nice to meet you.
Aunt Hilda looked him up and down
slowly, one eye narrowed.

Then a smile lifted her face,
and she said: *Good, Lottie. This is good.*
It is nice to have a friend.

DEAD

We went to the shed,
entered the dark womb of it,
the fusty fug of it.

I flicked the light, and my creatures
were illuminated
and so was Jeffrey's big smile.

His eyes shone—
the oily liquid of them
made my heart leap.

He stood for a long time,
his gaze travelling over
fur and feathers, beaks and claws.

His smile slowly closed.
Eventually, he said:
They're all dead.

His eyes, gentle and quizzical,
turned to mine.
Why do you keep them?

I felt my heart tighten
and slump.
I thought he'd understand.

I keep them because I love them.
I keep them because
they are beautiful.

And then I surprised myself and said:
I keep them because
they remind me of Mother.

MOTHER MEMORY II

She is lying on my small bed
crying—quietly, softly.

I stand and stare at her
wet face, her wet hair.

I touch the smooth skin of her cheek.
She opens her swollen eyes,

then gathers me up,
folds me into a warm, damp hug.

I smell her perfume,
feel the beat of her heart.

Adrianna, Adriaaanna.
Where are you? Adrianna.

Father gently calls from some dark
other part of the house.

REMEDY

Wolfgang, Charlotte needs
an interest, a hobby.
Something to occupy her time.

Why do I need a hobby? I asked.

Father looked up from the morning paper.
First at Aunt Hilda,
then at me.

A hobby? He frowned.

Yes, Aunt Hilda said. *It will keep her busy.*

Father nodded. I chewed my toast.
I am busy, I said.

It will keep you out of trouble.

I am not in trouble.

Hush! You need something
to keep you busy—sport or something.

Leave it with me.
Father put down the paper
rose, kissed my head,
and left.

INVASION

The days warmed, and the shadows
beneath the robinia strengthened.

In the shed, the fusty
smell of death swelled.

One day, before school,
I flicked a small black ant

off the top
of the aquarium.

When I returned that afternoon
there was a thick trail of ants

climbing the shed wall.
Inside, the floor was a dark sea

and my poor creatures
writhed as if alive.

Ants marched up my legs
biting flesh.

I hit and slapped and swore
and the air reeked.

BURIAL

Father dug a hole at the base
of the apricot tree.

With gardening gloves
and kitchen tongs

he removed my
ant-infested creatures,

my beautiful,
spoiled specimens.

Placed them all
into the hole,

covered them
with dirt.

The sound of shovel
striking ground.

The sound of earth
layering earth.

Like a blow,
sunk my breath,

filled my heart
with the dead

weight of
death.

SOLITUDE

I did not go to school
the next day or the next.
I did not want to go
ever again.

I stayed in bed,
lay on my back and slept,
or stared
at the blank ceiling and

the dust motes
that swirled around,
catching light
from a crack in the curtain.

I watched them dance,
sparkle and glitter.
I longed to feel some
of that magic,

but I was weighed down, heavy.
I too had been buried
beneath a tonne of soil
in that mass grave.

DARK RECESSES

On the third day
I could hear the heated
but hushed voices
of Aunt Hilda and Father.

Father came into my room,
sat on my bed,
studied my face,
stroked my hair and said:

It is hard to lose
anything or
anyone
we are close to.

It is good to feel sad.
It is good to cry.
It is good to grieve.

Tears swelled in my eyes.
Father's voice was soft and gentle
and full of pain.

In his eyes I saw
what I felt.
It was as if I had travelled

the distance
to his heart,
to the dark recesses
of his grief.

He offered me his hand.
Come. Let us sit in the lounge,
in the chair by the window
with the sun.

A GIFT FROM AUNT HILDA

This is for you, Lottie.
Aunt Hilda sat next to me,
passed me a woven basket.
Girls need to know how to sew.

I took off the lid and inside were
coloured cottons,
multi-sized needles, a thimble
and a needle threader.

It is good to learn. It is useful.
She passed me some fabric
and an assortment of buttons.
We will start with these.

The buttons were easy to stitch.
The time passed quickly, and
Aunt Hilda was happy.
You are good with the thread.

She showed me how to sew
a running stitch,
a back stitch,
a basting stitch.

My favourites were the
hemming stitch and
the invisible stitch.
My work was fine and neat.
I did not dislike
this small labour,
this benign act.
It buoyed me, and

for some time
it was all that I did:
stitch, stitch
stitch.

FATHER'S REMEDY I

A blackbird lay on a table.
Its orange beak
and sleek black feathers
shone under a spotlight.

An array of tools and materials
were assembled next to the bird:
a scalpel, silver scissors,
a needle and thread,
cotton wool and straw
and a dish holding
tiny black beads.

The man sliced the belly,
pulled out pink innards
peeled the wings
and body from the bones,
scooped out cerebral matter,
and removed the eyes
and tongue
until it was a formless
feather jacket.

And then he rebuilt the bird:
filled its body and breast
and eye sockets,
wired the wings,
stitched the wound and
mounted the little feet on a branch.

TAXIDERMY II

I could not think of anything
other than that beautiful bird
as I sewed on buttons
and stitched fabric
for Aunt Hilda.

Wolfgang! she had cried
last night over dinner
when I told her of the magical man
who brought the blackbird
back to life.

It was like a remaking,
a re-creation, a reinvention.

Father smiled at me
from his chair,
his knife and fork glinting.

Wolfgang! That is ghoulish.
This is not the solution.

Aunt Hilda waved a ladle in the air.
She is a girl. A girl!
What were you thinking?

RAINBOW

On the circular side table
the button box sat,
as I unpicked, unpicked, unpicked
and restitched, restitched
until perfect.

A bright strip of light
lit up the faded shirt
on my lap. There was a sudden
loud *smack!*

A drip of blood from my thumb,
a needle prick.
Did the window crack?
On the pane of glass
was a dark smear.

I sucked my thumb,
drew out more blood
and a metallic taste.
I watched a dark drip
slip slowly down the windowpane.

A reddish tinge
mixed with the green and white
stain of bird shit.
Outside, on the ground,
lay a rainbow lorikeet.

It was warm to hold.
Its eyes were closed.
I lifted its downy-feathered chest
to my cheek, but
could feel no heartbeat.

IMPLEMENTS

When the bird was boxed
under my bed,
Annie and I collected the implements,
tools of the trade:
tweezers, fabric scraps,
needle and thread,
sharp sewing scissors.

That night,
while Father was dozing
in front of the television,
when Aunt Hilda
had gone home,
Annie and I slipped into the study
in search of a knife.

We closed the door,
flicked on the light,
silently opened drawers,
until we found
the wood-encased
folded pocketknife
with its shiny razor tip.

MIDNIGHT I

When the house settled
and father's soft snores
moved from lounge
to bedroom,
we lay down a sheet,
set up our tools,
slid the boxed bird from
under the bed,
lifted the corpse
onto our makeshift
operating table.

We cut and sliced,
gouged,
pulled and tugged,
disembowelled.
There was some fluid,
a little dried blood.

We balled fabric
to stuff the cavity,
threaded the needle and sewed
the newly formed,
strangely figured shape.

When the bird was upright
its blue head
flopped heavily.

Its flaming chest
was unevenly puckered.
Its wings and legs
had no strength.
It eyes, red-rimmed,
had lost their sheen.

It was not beautifully remade;
it was awkwardly dead.

A FLARE OF LIGHT

School was a fog; my head
leaden from lack of sleep
lolled on the desk.

All day the little corpse,
the grotesque mutation,
fluttered through my thoughts.

I wanted to open it up,
to begin again,
unsew, unstuff, repeat.

I thought about the stages
of the taxidermy demonstration,
focused on the details.

Mr Morris droned on
about elements and compounds
and ignited a ribbon of magnesium,

and in that flare of light,
there was a flash of memory—
I must lighten the head,

remove the tongue,
scoop out the brain,
then remodel, restuff, restitch

the crumpled little bird
that lay in its box
beneath my bed.

BLOOD I

On the walk home from school
Annie and I passed a cluster
of bottlebrush trees.
Their fallen flowers created
perfect red circles
like pools of blood.

The afternoon was warm.
Fat dark clouds skimmed the sky.
Annie sniffed the air
like some albino wolf.
There will be rain tonight,
she said. *A storm is coming.*

We studied the birds:
sparrows, galahs, magpies.
We watched the way they moved—
their waddle, their flit, their hop,
the stretch of their wings
and the way they cocked their heads.

I thought of my mangled lorikeet.
It is a raggedy bird
full of dead cotton.

You need wire and sawdust
and beads for the eyes.

Annie was right. I needed
materials, more tools.
We will rummage the shed
when we get home,
Annie said. *We will raise*
that bird from the dead.

BLOOD II

We avoided Aunt Hilda,
dropped our bags
at the back door and
headed for the shed.

We fumbled through
metal drawers,
sifted through items
in boxes and trays.

We found a coil of wire,
pliers, sharp tweezers,
some fine sawdust,
but no little beads for the eyes.

We stowed them all
in my schoolbag,
opened the back door,
entered the laundry.

There in the sink
waiting to be washed
was our surgical sheet, stained
with the bird's blood.

BLOOD III

We tiptoed through the house
to my room.

We passed the kitchen
like silent kittens.

We headed to my bedroom
to dump my bag,

to check under the bed
for the box and the bird.

Lottie? Is that you?
The kitchen door swung open.

Light flooded the hall.
My heartbeat exploded in my head.

Lottie. I turned and faced
Aunt Hilda's looming shape.

Lottie. Come. Come.
I followed her into the kitchen.

Sit. Sit, she said and I scanned
the room for my boxed bird.

I sat. I swallowed. I waited.
I found the sheet, she said.

She rose up, engulfed me,
crushed me in a long moist hug.

You are now a young lady.
A woman. We must talk.

BLOOD IV

I placed the sanitary napkins,
the pads, on my bed,

bent down, dragged out
the cardboard box.

The bird was safe,
but smelled not-quite fresh.

We must excavate the head
before the ants come.

Aunt Hilda's talk about menses,
of wombs and babies and monthly blood

churned my stomach and filled me
with a dark-shadowed dread.

I picked up a thick napkin,
felt its softness between my fingers,

flicked open Father's pocketknife and sliced
into the pad's soft white flesh.

DINNER

Outside the storm had arrived,
thunder grumbled.

Rain drummed on the roof,
trees thrashed the windows.

But inside, there was a stillness,
a calmness. At the dining table

there was the gentle laying down
of china and cutlery.

I was not called to help.
I was called to eat.

Father smiled as he chewed,
called me *Young lady*.

Aunt Hilda hummed and nodded at me
as I ate hungrily.

She excused me from the dishes,
told me to rest on my bed,

whispered to Father that now
All will be well. Change is here.

MIDNIGHT II

We set up our surgical tools,
placed the bird on a fresh sheet
and began our work—
unpicking stitches,
pulling out the clump of fabric,
turning the feathery carcass
inside out to expose
the base of the skull,
scooping out the brain,
the cerebral matter,
little by little
till the eggshell skull
was empty.

The grey pink tongue,
strangely shaped
with barbs,
was stubborn,
but we tweezed it, tugged it out.
We had no beads to replace
the small red eyes
so we left them.
The body we filled with
wads of white downy cotton
from Aunt Hilda's
menstrual pads.

ALIVE

At 2.00 a.m.
the lorikeet was almost
alive.

Its wings were wired
for flight.
Its head was erect.

We lay it down and
climbed between the sheets
to go to sleep.

In the morning Aunt Hilda allowed
a day off school
to rest.

MOTHER MEMORY III

Her hair flows down her back
shining blue-black in the light
from the morning sun.

Oma is at the sink, washing
carrots and cabbage
pulled from the garden.

I gaze up at Mother.
The window squares
sit brightly in her eyes.
There's no room on her lap
so I lean against
her full-moon belly and feel

the soft drum of her voice
and her heart through her chest
where my ear rests.

Her ghost-white arm is wrapped
around me. The other hand strokes
my unborn sister.

She looks into my eyes
and her red lipstick lips
turn into a smile.

SUMMER AT OMA'S

Annie and I stared out
at the blaze of sea,
the blue bowl of sky,
the dark shadows falling down
yellow-grassed slopes, and
at magpies panting in trees.
The leaves of the gums mimicked
the sound of the beach.

Outside, the hot dry northerly
whipped up our hair.
Annie's glittered like tinsel.
Our thongs flip-flopped across
dry, dusty paddocks.
The sun stung our skin and
squinted our eyes.

We carried a silver bucket
to the orchard to pick apricots
from the netted trees.
We plucked soft warm globes
in the sweet-scented air
till the bucket was heavy
and our stomachs were full.

On the way back to the cottage,
beneath the gnarly almond tree,
Annie spied the hollowed-out hull
of a stumpy-tail lizard—
no eyes, no tongue, no innards.
Its carcass like cardboard,
its mouth ajar, its tail curled
as if fighting to the death.

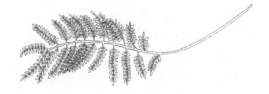

PRESERVATION III

The kitchen was a bubble
of boiling pots and kettles.
In the syrupy air
we washed and stoned the fruit,
our faces slick with sweat.

When the jars were full,
lined up neatly in the pantry,
when dinner had been eaten
and dishes washed, we went out
into the cooling afternoon.

The sea was a silver strip.
A bright round moon was rising
above the wheaty paddock.
Pink-tinged clouds followed us
as we searched for bodies.

Three eastern greys
grazing in the paddock,
one with a joey,
looked up and bounded away.
Fence wire twanged in their wake.

A murder of crows
caw-cawed up high.
Their black bodies
swirled like soot against
a backdrop of cloudy sky.

To the west, a wedge-tailed eagle
hovered and circled,
hovered and circled,
riding the remains
of the day's thermals.

Annie snatched my hand.
Let's see, she said, and we ran
beneath the circling bird,
and there on the ground
was a brown hare.

Its body still soft.
It was wildly beautiful, with
its black-tipped ears
as long as a kangaroo's
and its dead eyes open.

It was clear of marks,
there was no blood.
We dusted off ants,
shooed flies, carried
it carefully

back to the cottage, where
to preserve it
we lovingly wrapped it
in plastic and
put it in the freezer.

FIRE I

The northerly was back by morning.
The air was heated like a furnace;
the saplings were bending,
their branches stretching like children
reaching for mothers.

The long grass on the hillside
rippled like a yellow sea.
It was too hot to stay outside,
so I played solitaire with Annie
in the cool dark house.

At noon we ventured out
into the white-hot light.
Dark clouds billowed
on the hill. Annie sniffed.
A storm is coming. A fire storm.

Lottie! Oma shrieked
Warum ist das Kaninchen hier.

Annie and I rushed inside.
Smoke, Oma! On the hill.

Why is this rabbit here?
The hare's frozen face stared
behind the plastic.

Oma, there's a fire!
There is smoke. Big smoke!
Her eyes widened. *Where?*
She lifted her long black skirt
and we hurried out behind her.

FIRE II

The smell of smoke
was stronger,
the cloud closer
and blacker.
The heat intensified.
The wind
blustered hotly.

We followed Oma
up the hill
behind the house.
And there it was—
red flame, black smoke—
coming our way.

The sky rained
black ash;
red embers whirled and swirled.

Some faded, some landed
leaving dark marks
in the yellow grass.

Wasser! Oma yelled
over the roar and crackle.
Water! Wasser! Water!

We galloped
down the slope
back to the house
to find buckets and the hose.

FIRE III

Black smoke billowed,
the day darkened,
the dam greyed,
trees ignited.

We threw water,
doused spots of fire,
ran from one to the other,
choking on the acrid air,
until Oma's blackened hands
yanked us back into the house.

We cowered in a dark corner.
Oma's prayers swirled
around us
like flaming embers, until
the wail of sirens,
the flash of fire-truck lights.

Firefighters lifted, lugged,
hauled, tugged
the reeled-up hose,
sprayed jets of water
at the house,
at the garden,
at the flaming
overhanging gums.

MO(U)RNING

The hill was dark stubble,
the air, acrid.
Trees smouldered;
streams of smoke drifted
and curled
like smoke signals,
silently echoing
Oma's despair.

The gums,
empty of birdsong,
were jagged sticks
of charcoal.

Oma muttered
German prayers
and curses,
as we crunched over
the scorched
vegetable patch and
the fruitless orchard.

She wept at the sight
of the toppled henhouse
and the scatter
of burnt feathers.

FROM THE ASHES

Father's blue Valiant
emerged through a haze
of low-slung smoke.
The engine rumbled eerily
up the birdless track.

The wrench of handbrake
and thud of car door
echoing around the valley
intensified the bleak
black moonscape.

He walked the grounds,
hands in pockets,
mouth tight,
boots turning over
charred remains
of trees and other debris.
Occasionally he squatted
and stared at something,
with hands knotted together.

At last, he came into the house,
placed an arm around
Oma's shoulders, and
squeezed briefly,
releasing from her
a deep-throated sob.

SEASCAPE

There was no electricity,
no water in the tank,
no chickens to feed.
The house reeked of smoke.

Oma salvaged
the food in the fridge.
Packed a big black bag
and a box.

Annie and I collected our
smoke-scented clothes,
the thawed-out hare
and the hollowed-out lizard.

We sat in the Valiant
and leaned our heads against
the sun-heated window
after our sleepless night.

We watched the sea glitter,
and the waves roll and roll,
as the car wound its way
along the south coast.

Oma's box sat between us,
gently tipping with each turn.
The photos inside slid
this way and that.

Annie and I shuffled through
black-and-white snaps
of Opa and Father and Uncle Bernard
in their German uniforms

and image after image
of Father with Mother,
their faces as grim
as the charred hillside.

GRAINY MEMORIES

There are photos of all of us
at different ages and stages.

Many I have seen,
like the one in Father's study
of Father, Uncle Bernard and Opa
with those Japanese men
holding up leafy vegetables—
beetroot, maybe.

We study it,
Annie and I,
taking in the dark tones—
the smiling men
looking pleased
with their produce.
Sifting through again,
we find Aunt Hilda
when she was young,
holding a small child.

That is you! Annie says.
There with your dark hair,
your chubby finger in your mouth,
and your head resting
on Aunt Hilda's shoulder.

See how she holds you.
See how she smiles.

Suddenly I was filled with warmth
for my aunt
who was always there trying
to fill the space
that Mother left behind.

OMA

When we arrived home
the sun was sinking
and the sky bled
yesterday's smoke.

Aunt Hilda hugged Oma,
gathered her bent bird-frame
into her own generous bulk
and muttered German words.

Dinner was sombre.
Father frowned at his plate,
chewed methodically, robotically.
I ate quickly to escape

Aunt Hilda's fussing
and the awkward, anxious presence
of Oma, whose hair and cheeks
were smudged with ash.

Later, Aunt Hilda made room for Oma,
emptied Mother's drawers and wardrobe.
Carried bundle after bundle of clothes
and shoes out to the shed.

Oma followed her this way and that.
The scent of wood smoke drifted behind her.
She sighed and clucked, and rolled out
the long sounds of Mother's name.

I have told him. Aunt Hilda shook her head.
Wolfgang, let her go. But he will not.
It is hard. Too hard, I know.
But we will help. It is a step.

SCENT

Annie and I rummaged through
Mother's displaced bundles
and breathed in the scent
of long ago.

She was still there.
Her particles embedded
in the weave of cloth.
The indentation of her body
pressed into her clothes
and shoes and belts.

We tried to read those hollows
and grooves, the depressions,
the scuff marks,
the wear and tear,
but they were as indecipherable
as those ancient hieroglyphs.
As impenetrable
as an Egyptian tomb.

I pulled on layer after layer of her:
underwear, stockings,
shirts and skirts,
coat and shoes.
I wrapped myself in her,
folded myself up
until it felt
like a warm hug.

In the pocket of her coat
I found an envelope
folded into a small fat square
with 'Wolf' printed
in a back-slanted hand.

We unfolded once, twice, three times
until Father's full name appeared.
We opened the flap,
exposed the yellowed seal,
the stain of red lipstick
and the jingle jangle
of a diamond ring and
a wedding band.

THE LIVING DEAD

Annie jangled the rings
danced around the room, sang:
Jack and Jill went up the hill
to fetch a pail of water.
Jill fell down and broke her crown
and Jack came tumbling after.

We are living a nursery rhyme.
When Mother died
poor Father survived, but
his heart breaks, smashes, shatters
every day and always will.
He is the living dead.

THE LIZARD AND THE HARE

At midnight when the house was quiet,
when Oma had settled
into a fitful slumber,
we crept past her open door
and entered the study.

The thawed hare had warmed.
We couldn't risk
Aunt Hilda sniffing it out.
We needed to hollow it like the lizard,
remove the innards, disembowel.

We needed a longer, sharper knife.
The pocketknife was too short,
the skin of the hare too thick.
We'd blunted the blade
on our jewelled bird.

We flicked on the desk lamp,
filled the room with a yellow glow
and hunted through drawers
until we found Father's fishing knife,
its blade glinting in the light.

Back in our room, we operated
like surgeons.
Sliced open belly,
removed entrails,
scooped out brain & bone & eyes.

At 3.00 a.m. we wrapped
the slippery mass in an old dress,
rolled it up into a neat parcel,
tiptoed down the garden path,
and placed it in the incinerator.

MOTHER MEMORY IV

They carry the box,
the tiny coffin,
down the aisle
of the church.

Mother moans
and Oma sobs.

The coffin is shiny
and as white
as Mother's face.

Her dark-circled eyes
loom like giant
black moons.

RESURRECTION I

Lottie! Zeit aufzustehen! Up, up!
I opened my eyes.
Strong sunshine
seeped through the blinds.
Oma peered at me through
a criss-cross of lines.

I yawned and stretched
and Oma smiled.

The lines in her face
changed shape and direction
and I caught a glimpse of
small white teeth.

Up, up! Beeil dich! Hurry!
We are going out!
She walked to the door,
turned, sniffed the air,
frowned.
Then continued on her way.

Father was reading the *Advertiser*,
a steaming cup of coffee
at his elbow.
He glanced up and nodded
as I entered the room.

I sat at the table and ate,
listened to the sound of my teeth
crushing cornflakes.
I thought of the skinned hare
and wondered how I might tackle
the resurrection.

Lottie, Father said,
nodding at my half-eaten cereal.
Hurry now. We are going
for a long drive to the Riverland.

COUNTRY

Annie and I played
I Spy with My Little Eye
in the back of the car.
We passed S and T (spindly trees)
Y and P (yellow paddocks)
and G and S (many grey sheep).

Oma and Father sat silently
side by side, until
Oma clucked or tutted,
adding little bird nods
to something she saw
and Father grunted.

The road was dry dust, red rust.
The R (for river) snaked
in and out of view,
with reflections of chalky yellow cliffs
glittering in the water.

We stopped at Blanchetown
where the river was studded
with dead trees posing
like ballet dancers
playing Statues.

LUFF DIE

We drove on through Waikerie
to Wiggly Flat and
Kingston-on-Murray.
We followed long snaky roads
watched the RM's (River Murray's) brown water
slipping in and out of view.

Luff Die, Oma said. *Luff Die*.
A strange prickly stillness descended
as the car slowed and
Father flicked the indicator.
Tick-tick, tick-tick, tick-tick.
Luff Die. Oma pointed a twisted finger.

Luff Die—Love Die?
Luff Die—Love Dies?
Annie shrugged her thin shoulders,
chewed her bottom lip
till a bead of blood glistened
like a tiny jewel.

Father's frown filled
the rear-vision mirror.
Sharp vertical lines divided his eyebrows.
Oma muttered indecipherable words
in German and English
as we rolled along the dirt track.

LOVEDAY I

The car stopped at a fenced area.
Father opened the door,
eased himself out of his seat
and stared at the untidy scrub.

Oma hobbled around the car
shook her head. *Luff Die. Luff Die.*
He should not have been here.
Nor you, nor Bernard.

It has mostly gone. Our huts
have been carted away, Father said.
It's still here, Oma replied. *Still here.*
The sadness…die Traurigkeit.

I can feel it, Annie whispered.
The air is heavy with ghosts.
The birds sing only sad songs.
The ground swallowed many tears.

Oma wiped her eyes.
It was not always bad for us, Father said.
But it was unfair. Unjust.
Ja. Unjust. Oma repeated. *Ungerecht.*

LAKE BONNEY

From our upstairs window
at the Barmera Hotel
we watched Lake Bonney
change from blue to pink then red,
mirroring the sky at sunset.
Sailor's delight, Annie said.
But in the morning, it's a warning.

We rose early and
walked the lake with Father.
The air was already hot,
the heated sand warmed our feet.
Broken eggshells and tiny tracks
from baby turtles
littered the shore.

Flocks of pelicans,
all angles and sharp edges,
unfolded themselves
and drifted across the smooth water
with coots and cormorants.
All of them honking, grunting
and gabbling.

Why did we stop at Loveday?
I asked Father as I followed him
along the sandy path,
his back peppered with flies.

It is a place of many memories.
Oma wanted to visit.
For her memories...of Opa.

Of Opa? I asked, baffled.
I thought back to Oma's words—
He should not have been here—
and waited for Father's response.
He stopped, turned to the lake,
and stared at the water for a long time,
before turning back to the path
and walking on in silence.

CORKS

Later, Annie and I bobbed
like corks
on our foam surfboards.

The womb-like lap of the lake
was like Mother's soft heartbeat.

Father stood to attention
on the shoreline, watching.

The sun dried and tightened
the skin on our backs.

Annie's bone-white body glowed
and her wet hair turned the colour
of scorched wheat.

Mine, wet and dark,
had a tinge of burgundy.
My skin was the colour of dirt.

We held hands and drifted
to the middle of the lake
where we could hear
Father's distress call:
Lotti…Lotti…Lottie!

We slow-paddled back
to the narrow shoreline,
to Father's troubled face.

I told you to stay close.
Close to the shore.

His gaze held mine until
I lowered my eyes.

You should not swim out
that far on your own.

Sorry, Father.
I am a good swimmer.

Yes, Lottie, but I am not.
And I worry.

Father's voice was as raspy
as sandpaper.

Come, get dressed.
We are going for a drive—
to the cemetery.

BARMERA CEMETERY

Oma walked up and down
and turned around in circles
like a little lost dog.

It was here. Somewhere. Ach.
They buried them all. Buried him.
There should be a Denkmal, a plaque.

Buried who? I asked Father.
Father did not look up.

He stared down at an unmarked grave,
slipped his hands into his pockets.

Opa was buried here, somewhere.
Later exhumed, reburied near the farm.

Tears trickled down the little ravines
in Oma's cheeks.

Father wrapped an arm around
her bony shoulders.

The fire. The birds. My birds.
He is not here to see. At least, at least.

THE TURNING OF THE BONES

I remembered the word
'exhumed' from school.
Annie nodded. *Exhume:*
to dig up, unearth, disentomb.

Mr Morris told us of the rituals
and customs of the Madagascans
who celebrate their dead
in a ceremony called
the Turning of the Bones.

The cloth-wrapped bodies
are exhumed,
sprayed with wine or perfume
and danced with
while a band plays lively tunes.

Then he said: *The traditions of our*
own Aboriginal people differ
depending on clan and location—
some have a smoking ceremony.

We all turned to Jeffrey
whose eyes were empty
and unblinking, and his body
as still and calm as always.

Some lie their dead on a raft
cover them with native plants

and when the bodies have decomposed
they collect and scatter the bones.

Some people keep a bone.
Sometimes in grief they cut themselves.
They moan and wail, and as a show of respect
they do not speak the names of their dead.

LOVEDAY II

I imagined my Opa,
my grandfather
who I knew only
in black and white,
in old photographs—
his grave face,
his grey uniform,
his metallic gun,
his shiny medals.

I imagined Opa lying
beneath the earth.
Now he would be bones
and bits of cloth.
The earth, the worms,
the insects, the microbes

would have consumed him:
his skin, his muscle,
the finely shaped nails
of his fingers and toes.

In my mind I resurrected him.
I built him up,
filled him with stuffing,
dusted the dirt from his bones.
Remodelled the flesh,
the muscle, the sinew.
Rewired, reconstructed,
resurrected, rewound,
revised the present.
Rewrote the past.

THE APOSTLES

Father wandered away
with hands behind his back, followed
by a group of chattering birds—apostles.

He weaved in and around gravestones:
some tall (monumental), some small (inconsequential):
grey stone, black stone, and polished pink marble.

Eventually he stood at the foot of a grave
and said, *I remember this man, Jimmy James.*
He was a good man. An Aboriginal tracker.

He captured eight escapees
from the Loveday camp during the war,
then contracted tuberculosis and died.

I thought of Jeffrey.
I missed him and his quiet ways.
His gentle eyes and voice.

The apostles gathered at Father's feet.
Hushed now, their dark grey heads still,
as if they were listening to his thoughts.

QUESTIONS

Oma stood in her corner
of the cemetery; Father stood in his.

Both heads were bowed,
deep in thought.

*They are the colour
of grief,* Annie said.

I did not know what she meant
by colour, but did not ask.

I had too many other questions
running through my head.

What did father mean: escapees?
Why did Jimmy James track them?

Was there a smoking ceremony
for Jimmy James?

Was his body laid out on a raft?
Were his bones scattered?

Did his people keep his bones,
moan, cut themselves?

Or are his bones, here,
in this plot, in a wooden box?

Is it okay for his grave to be named?
Will that disturb his spirit?

What of Loveday? What is Loveday?
Why were Father and Opa there?

Why was Opa buried here?
Why was he exhumed?

When was he moved?
I felt disordered, unmoored.

SKIRTING LAKE BONNEY

Father and I followed a ragged path
around the lake. My pace swift,
his long-legged, leisurely.

The sun slept behind woolly clouds.
The lake was flat and still and silvery
like a fine piece of silk.

Why? I asked Father, *was Opa buried here*
in Barmera? Why so far from Oma?
And what is Loveday?

Father took a deep breath
and a long pause…

Loveday was a camp,
an internment camp
for Germans, Japanese and Italians
during the War.

It was a place for internees
and prisoners of war.

It was my turn to pause.
Prisoners of war?

Why were you prisoners?
What did you do?
Were you bad? All of you together?

We are German and we—
Germany was
at war with Australia.

And Opa? Father, what happened to Opa?
Why was he buried in Barmera?

Father stopped walking,
looked out across the smooth lake
to the skeletal trees on the other side.

Opa was old, his health not good.
The nights were very, very cold;
he got pneumonia and passed away.

They buried all the prisoners
who died at Loveday
here in Barmera. And moved them later.

Father's blue eyes moistened, and
the blue deepened and deepened
into cool, aquamarine lakes.

DANCING WITH GHOSTS

We ate dinner at right angles
in silence
around the teak-veneer table.

The hotel dining room was empty,
but for a couple sitting in a corner
holding hands.

The thick red carpet absorbed
the chink and clink
of our plates and cutlery.

I watched the lemonade bubbles
in my glass rise and burst.
Rise and burst.

Father sipped his beer,
wiped froth from his beard.
Oma said: *This steak is good, ja?*

Father smiled and grunted his
approval, but his eyes were focused
on the couple in the corner.

You see them, Annie whispered.
She is dark, he is fair—
Just like Mother and Father.

It was true, Annie was right.
Father sees it too, she said.
His head is dancing with ghosts.

MURDER I

In the morning
Father said we could not swim,
so we walked the lake perimeter
hunting for turtles and eggs,
but found none.

When we walked back,
Annie and I watched
a clatter of cockatoos,
a racket, a rattle, a jangle, a clank,
a clash, a bangle, a mangle
of flapping wings,
flared sulphur crests,
beaks pecking at one of their own
they had dragged off the road.

They nudged, screeched and tugged,
but the cockatoo lay still.
A battered wing
erect
like a broken flag.

One nestled into the body,
lay down next to its mate.

Murder, Annie said. *It was a murder.*
She nodded at the road,
to the passing cars.

We stood and stared and wept,
for the death of the beautiful bird,
for the death of their union,
for Father and Mother,
for Oma and Opa.

LIKE SLAVES

In the afternoon we returned
to Loveday.
Father drove the car around the grounds
and pointed things out to Oma,
who drank it in,
nodded and nodded
and swallowed back gasps.

Over there we grew poppies.
Here, the piggery.
Vegetables in that paddock.
The train transported prisoners
and produce.

You worked hard? Oma asked.
Yes, said Father.
Your vater, he work hard?
Yes, he worked too.
Wie Sklaven—Like slaves.

No, not like slaves, said Father.
We did not have to work.
He liked to be in the garden.
It helped with the boredom—
the long, long days
away from you.
It eased us into sleep
on those freezing nights.

Ach! The freezing.
Oma shook her head.
He should not have been here.
It broke his heart.
This is how he die.
You should not have been here.
We are good Germans.
We are good people.

Father slipped one hand
in his pocket
and the other around
Oma's shoulder
and stared ahead at
the empty land.

INCINERATE

We arrived home beneath
a sickle moon
and faint suburban stars.

Aunt Hilda opened the door,
greeted us with crossed arms,
a frown, a grimace, slitted eyes.

Father raised his eyebrows
in question. Oma clucked but
without concern.

Annie and I got a slow nod
and we knew it was about us.
We yawned, headed to bed.

We lay on the bedspread
in the heated room and listened
to Aunt Hilda's unhappy grumbling.

The words were mumbled, jumbled sounds
but I caught my name
and other words: *She, You, Must.*

I placed an ear against the wall,
listened to the muffled voices and the bang
and boom of my own heartbeat.

Look! Tell me this is normal.
Here...here...she is a ghoul,
Frankenstein. It is wrong.
The curtains rose and fell
like lungs as the window breathed
hot air around the room.

Father's low voice rumbled:
You found it in the incinerator?

Yes! She is killing and skinning.

MIRROR DREAM

Birds fly over the dam.
Their image reflected in the water—
black on gold
tinged rose by the setting sun.

Black and yellow cockatoos, Annie says.
Funeral birds, says Oma.
Ghouls, corrects Aunt Hilda.
Ghoulish girls.

The birds fly circles,
form a spiral pattern
like dark sky dancers.
Bad omen. Good omen.

Suddenly they change shape.
Their slow wing-beat quickens.
Their soft song hardens—
Ark-ark, ark-ark.

Crows, Annie says. Floating on her back,
her hair stained blood-red
by the sinking sun.
A murder, she says. *It's a murder.*

THE BURNING I

I was jolted awake
by the smell of smoke.
Disoriented—
I thought I was back
with the bushfire.

But we were home and
the curtain was billowing
warm smoky air.

I rubbed my eyes,
opened the curtains wide,
and there was Aunt Hilda
at the back of the garden
beside the incinerator.

Dark clotted clouds
drifted upwards
and the smell of hair
drifted inside.

I leapt out of bed.
Got down on hands and knees.
Felt for the box
but it was gone!

I raced outside, screamed.
No, no, no. Where is it?
What have you done!

It is gone, burnt, Charlotte,
Aunt Hilda shouted
over the crackle.

I snatched the stick from her hand.
Leaned into the fire,
stabbed at the flames.

She tried to wrestle it back,
tried to pull me away.
But I would not give up.

I could see the hare
looking back at me
through the smoke.

The lizard curled
and shrivelled next to it.
I poked at the flames,

breathed bitter smoke,
coughed and coughed,
felt pain in my hands.

My hair crackled and sizzled
in the radiant heat
but I hooked my precious creature,

and tossed the blackened fur
out of the flames
onto the faded, dry grass.

THE BURNING II

What is going on?
Father strode out of the house.

Aunt Hilda stood with her
hands on her hips.

It is for her own good.
It is not healthy to kill and skin.

Oma appeared beside Father,
a hand to her mouth, her brow crinkled.

Fire? she said. *Ach, the smoke.*
Why is the rabbit burning? Put it out.

Smoke drifted in long tendrils
from the hare.

I'd rescued it from the hawk
and then from the bushfire.

I'd rescued it from its own
disintegration.

And here it was, its pelt ruined,
blackened, half-charred.

There was nothing I could do
to resurrect it now.

Its soft tawny fur,
its elegant long ears,

its sweet nose and cotton tail—
singed, blackened, burnt beyond repair.

Aunt Hilda lifted it by an ear,
tossed it back into the flames.

It is gone, finished, final.
For your own good.

And the others, she said,
the parrot, that lorikeet, and the lizard.

My heart skipped a beat;
the world blurred.

The pain in my hands
moved to my chest.

My beautiful rainbow lorikeet—
my jewel, my treasure.

All that work, all that beauty
gone, burnt to cinders.

BANDAGES

Oma iced my hands,
clucked and tutted.
Stroked my hair,
tucked a strand
behind my ear.
Wiped my tears.

I did not care
about the burns.
I did not care
about the pain.
I cared only for
my lost creatures.

MURDER II

A murder, Annie said.
It was murder.

She killed our creatures.
Our beautiful creatures.

And she put Mother
and her belongings here in the shed.

I dug to the bottom
of the cardboard box,

pulled the stole, the fox,
from its hidey-hole.

Slipped it on, around my neck
and wept and sobbed
and wept.

MEAT

At the dinner table
Aunt Hilda hovered
quietly,
uncertainly,
as Oma and Father
fussed over me.

It was hard to eat
with bandages
thick and tightly wound.
My mummified hands
were stiff with pain.
The food on my plate
cut into bite-size pieces.

I could only eat
a few slices of carrot.
The meat, the chicken
reminded me
of charred hare
and lorikeet.

It brought fresh tears
that would not cease,
and I knew I would never
again eat meat.

I fled the dining table,
fled the worried looks
and pleas.

MOTHER MEMORY V

She is sitting
at the kitchen table,
a dark silhouette
against the bright day
streaming in
through the window.

Her body is bent,
her arms thin.
Like a cubist rendition
of herself,
all squares, rectangles, triangles.
There is never a smile.

When I climb into her lap
I feel her hip bones,
her jutting ribs,
her pointed elbows.

Everything is sharp,
everything protrudes,
as if she is made
out of knives.

SILENCE I

There is power in silence—
in grief, in pain.
When you stop talking
people feel as if you cannot understand.
They talk about you
as if you are not there.
I wondered if this is what happened
to Mother.

Aunt Hilda spoke to Father:
She is hardly eating.
She will not eat her meat.
She will not look at me.
I am worried, Wolfgang.
What shall we do? What can I do?
Let's leave her be, Father said gently.
Perhaps time will heal.

I did not respond, did not talk,
did not want to talk.
There was nothing to say.
There was nothing to do;
nothing could undo.
Oma took me back to the farm
while she settled in,
but we did not speak.

She seemed to understand
my pain, my loss,
my lack of connection.
She treated me like a little dog—
stroked my hair,
fed me regularly
and talked to me.
Did not expect answers.

FIRE GROUND

The land was regenerating,
repairing itself.

Bright green shoots
sprouted from the black gums.

It had rained while we were away.
The dam had deepened,

the rainwater tank half-filled,
tufts of spiky grass could be seen

and the birds were singing
from the trees again.

The trilling of the blackbirds,
the warbling of the magpies,

the yarking of the crows—
the songs of Oma's birds

were the only sounds
I wanted to hear.

A FEBRUARY EVENING

The air was fresh, crisp.
The sun sleeping
under a soft tawny blanket
of cloud the colour
of a skinned hare.

I stroked the fur stole
warming my neck.
Mother was never far.
She was close
in those short soft strands.

I sat in the dirt and watched
Oma cluck and fuss
over her new chickens.
They scratched in the dust
while Father rebuilt the coop.

Oma placed one in my lap.
Liebkosen? Cuddle, she said.
The chicken pecked
at my sleeping fox,
then settled neatly into my lap.

Father nodded at Oma
and smiled as I stroked the bird.
Then he strode away, hands in pockets,
grim-faced to watch the day
sink sadly into the dam.

ARS MORIENDI—
THE ART OF DYING I

Annie and I wandered
around the farm,
left Father and Oma
to their quiet breakfast,

walked the blackened landscape,
kept going to the road,
down the hill—down, down
towards the glittering sea.

The day was blustery
but not cold.
The stole warmed me.
The touch of Mother felt safe.

We stood on the shore
and listened to the sound of the ocean,
our shoes in our hands,
our jeans rolled to our knees.

We watched the waves roll in and out,
watched the foaming sea
make lacy patterns
across the sand.

The icy water rushed
over our feet,
dragged the sand beneath our toes
back out to sea.

We could go in, Annie said.
We could go for a swim.
We could fill our pockets
with stones and drown.

We stared across the ocean
to the horizon
where a small ship sat.
We could, but we won't.

ARS MORIENDI—
THE ART OF DYING II

We walked the windy shoreline
till the heaviness left our bones,
then turned towards the farm,
strolled up the hill.

Beneath a row of giant pine trees,
we came across the corpse
of a brushtail possum
stretched out on its side.

Eyes open so wide, it looked alive.
And then it moved—
its front paw and nose twitched
and it blinked, slowly.

I could see no wounds, no blood.
Perhaps it fell from the tree
or was hit by a car.
We sat beside it, wondering what to do.

And then it stretched its paw
as if it wanted us to hold its hand.
We watched and waited, did not touch.
Annie spoke gentle words—

Sweet possum, beautiful creature,
you are a gift, a treasure—

until the light left its eyes
and it passed quietly away.

THICKENING

The possum thickened
my sadness.
Its quiet death added
weight to my legs,
already heavy
with grief.

I cried all the way
back to Oma's.
The fox stole was moist
with tears
when we finally arrived.

Death is sad.
The dead are gone
but not forgotten,
said Annie.
We could go back,
collect the creature.

It was beautiful
and in good condition.
We could take it home,
remove the skin
remodel, stitch, resurrect—
bring it back from the dead.

I shook my head.
There was no point;
it would be futile,
with Aunt Hilda,
so we left it for nature
to slowly digest.

THE BONE YARD

At the gate of the farm
we detoured,
went to the cemetery instead.

Annie skipped her way there,
her legs weightless—
the possum forgotten.

She carried everything lightly,
as only the dead
and the innocent can.

It is not a sad place.
There are bones buried, yes,
but there are birds
and cows and lizards
and crickets.

Annie was right. Life was all around:
cows grazed on yellow fields,
blue wrens squilled and flitted and hopped,
pigeons and magpies perched
on fence wire and tombstones,
and galahs creaked and squabbled
in the treetops.

The marble slabs
with their small square stones
propped up like pillows
resembled long lines of beds,
as if people had just come
to sleep or rest.

LINING UP THE DEAD

Opa's gravestone was gunmetal marble
like the grey of his portraits,
the stone as cool to touch
as his Luger pistol.

Uncle Bernard was standing by,
as silent in death as in life.
He never said much more than
hello and goodbye to me.
Now it was only goodbye.

Mother's stone was a pink coral colour.
A tall monument,
as elegant and beautiful
and lonely in death
as she seemed in life.

The sadness swirled around her
and around us
in eddies of white sandy dust.

She's talking, Annie said,
and I wanted to believe her,
but the dust settled
and there were no answers at my feet
or in my head
about why she died, why she left.

Next to Mother, the small grave,
the tiny rectangle
with the little angel on
the polished white stone
brought fresh tears,
fresh grief.

Annie poked me. *Don't be sad...*
She skipped around the tombstones.
It is only death. It is not the end!
We all die. We all die.
It's a part of life.

But I could not share
Annie's rosy thoughts.
I wanted to resurrect them all.
I wanted them back
breathing real air.
I wanted flesh and blood,
not ghosts.

OMA'S BOX OF MEMORIES

Take this box, these pictures, Oma said.
If there is another fire they burn.
What then? What have I got?
No more Fotos.
No more memories. All die.

Oma sat the box on my lap,
waved goodbye, and we drove up
the blackened track,
back to the city, back to Aunt Hilda
and the end of the holidays.

I looked through the photos,
one grim face after another
of Mother and Father, Oma and Opa.
Why are they all so sad?

Father smiled, pleased that I had spoken.
We did not want to leave
Germany, our Germany,
but we did not like the government,
so we came to Australia,
hoping for a good life.
We left family behind.

And then you were locked away?
Father's jaw clenched:
When the new war began, yes.
We were locked up in Loveday.

What of Mother and Oma?
Where were they?

Some women were sent to camps,
but your mother and Oma
worked on the land.

They stayed on their own?
On the farm?

Yes. There was no money.
There was no help.

And your mother
became very unwell.

ANNIE II

I shuffled through the box,
found a black-and-white photo
of me sitting on Annie's small lap:

Annie's hair shining whitely;
mine a flat dark shadow.

Her thin torso almost hidden
behind my plump little body.

Her stick thin arms
wrapped around my shoulders.

My mouth gnawing
a chubby index finger.

Her gappy grin, her pale lively eyes,
radiating zest and mischief,

and mine dark and round
beneath an uncertain frown.

CARTWHEELS I

Today the trees are full of flowers
and parrots.
Rainbow, musk and little lorikeets
hang from branches
like gaudy clowns,
squawking and chattering
as they strip the flowering gums,
leaving yellow pools
and blood-red shadows beneath.

A small cluster of corellas
and a dozen galahs
waddle in the middle of a grassy paddock.
Will the large flock come again?
Life is turning circles,
doing cartwheels around me,
and I am wandering alone
with the dead,
with Annie.

SCHOOL III

The first day of school
felt like a death.

The long school holidays
gone.

Back there with the kids
who didn't talk to me

was like being at a funeral
every day.

Thank God for Jeffrey.

CONTRAST

Jeffrey and I were the same
but different.
He was black, I was white.
He was male, I was female.
But we were both tall,
we were both thin
and quiet.
And each other's
only friend.

You've grown, he said
when he saw me.
It was true. I was taller
and I was different:
I had small breasts
and I had pimply bumps
on my chin and forehead.
Jeffery, too, was taller,
his limbs stronger,
his feet and hands larger.

We were both growing up
in our own ways,
together.

FAMILY HISTORY

We had to take photos of family
to school for Social Science
for a genealogy assignment.

I flicked through Oma's box of memories,
chose one of Opa and Father
both tall and straight and handsome
in their German uniforms.

And one of Mother, beautifully
wrapped in her long dark coat
wearing the fox stole;
her hair silky-black,
her face luminous.

And one of Oma with her arm
wrapped around a young Aunt Hilda,
who looked girlish and shy,
slender and pretty.

I slipped them in an envelope
along with the photo of me
sitting with Annie.

FAMILY I

Where are your photos? I asked.
I don't have any.
You don't have any photos?
Jeffrey shook his head.
I don't have any family.

What about the people you live with?
Aren't they your parents?
I thought Jeffrey was adopted.
He shook his head again.
They are nice people, but
they are not my family.

I asked him about Jimmy James,
but he did not know him.
I asked him if he knew how to track,
and he smiled a sad, upside-down smile.
I wish I could track back home.

FAMILY II

Jeffrey looked inside my envelope,
pulled out a photo and studied it.

That is me and Annie, I told him.
Annie is my sister.

He turned his gentle brown eyes
to mine and quietly said,
I didn't know you had a sister.

I stared at the photograph
for a long time, a lifetime.

She died.
She drowned in Oma's dam
when she was six.

The words fell from my mouth
as if tied to brick

plummeting, plummeting,
into deep, dark water.

WAR I

Others had brought photographs
of fathers and grandfathers
dressed in uniform.

But they were Australian
and British soldiers.

The kids in class said:
Your father is German
A Kraut.
Your grandfather
was in the Gestapo.
He was a Nazi.
He killed Jews.
You're a Kraut, a Nazi,
a traitor, an enemy.
You love Hitler!

He did not!
I do not!
It's not true.
We are peaceful Germans.

I did not tell them
about Loveday.

I did not tell them
that Father and Opa
were locked away.

OUTSIDERS

I did not fit in.
They called me a Kraut, a Nazi, Gestapo.
But I was born here,
my sister was born here,
my mother died here.
We will all die here.

My interest in ancient tombs
and mummies and dead things
did not help.
I was a freak, a vampire, a weirdo.
Aunt Hilda was right.

And Jeffrey's dark skin,
amid a sea of white,
made him an alien too.
In the country
of his ancestors.
They called him abo,
darky, boong,
black boy, nigger.

MY ANNIE

She took the small canoe,
untied the rope.
Pushed the little boat into the dam.

I cried and cried.
Annie why did you leave me?
Why did you die?

Because I loved the water and
that sweet little boat.
I loved the rhythm, the ripples,
the reflections.

I lay on the boat
with my fingers dangling,
feeling for fish.

When I stretched too far
the boat toppled,
tipped me in.

The water was a shock.
It was icy and deep.

I drank it in, panicked,
forgot how to swim.

DEATH AND JEFFREY

I asked Jeffrey about the dead.
I asked him about his customs,
about his people.

He didn't remember much,
just funerals
at the mission.

Whitefella funerals,
white folk sermons,
whitefella ways.

I remember some smoke,
and my mother and aunties
moaning.

But it was long time ago
and the memory is
like a wisp of smoke.

DEATH: A POEM

The hollowed-out hull
of a blue-tongue lizard.

Chickens charred
in a bushfire.

A heart attack or
a broken heart.

A small body
floating in a dam.

A long, dark,
deep depression.

Ash swirling
from an incinerator.

The smell of burning
on a hot breeze.

An internment camp.
A feeble body, a cold night.

A blue-born baby
and a bad placenta.

A birthday celebration—
thirteen today.

Breasts sprouting, limbs gangly,
a smear of blood.

WAR II

Aunt Hilda prepared
bratwurst and sauerkraut
for my birthday lunch,
which I would not eat.

I am not German.
I am Australian.
And I don't—
I won't—eat meat.

It was the first time
I had spoken to my aunt
since she cremated
my creatures.

You are German
and you will sit
and you will eat and
you will be normal.

I turned, walked out.
Leaving her with her hands
on her hips and her face
as purple as a cabbage.

DRESSED FOR DINNER

Father came home early from work
to take us all to dinner.
We were going to eat Swiss food
at a restaurant in the city.

I waited until he called, then emerged
wearing one of Mother's dresses,
her earrings, her perfume,
and the fox stole.

Aunt Hilda's eyes widened,
her mouth tightened,
at the sight of the curled creature
warming my neck.

Father, too, was stunned.
Lottie, dear Lottie. You look so very,
very beautiful.
You look exactly like your mother.

I smiled but there was sadness
and distance in his eyes.
I slipped on Mother's coat,
gathered myself into her arms.

A GIFT AND A CURSE

Your dark eyes
Your dark hair
The ruby lips, the shape
Of your face
Your everything
is hers—
Your mother's.
You are a gift
And a curse.

MORE GIFTS

Aunt Hilda gave me
the essentials: new underwear,
a flannelette nightgown
and perfumed soap.

Oma tucked my hair behind my ear.
Adrianna. You and she, just the same.
She gave me a photo of Mother.
Her beautiful sorrow held
in a gilt-edged frame.

There was still sadness in Father's eyes
when he passed me the gift-wrapped box.
Usually he gave me books,
but this was a camera:
a Praktica Super TL.

I hope you like it.
You seemed to like Oma's photos—
now you can make your own
box of memories.

I love it, Father. Thank you.
I stroked the leather case,
flicked through the instructions,
rattled the boxes of film.
I could not wait to try it.

SPELLS

When we stepped out into the chilly air
I put my hands into Mother's coat pocket
and there it was, almost forgotten.
The folded envelope.
On the way home,
I pulled it out.

I slipped the rings on my fingers,
rubbed and rubbed them,
as if they were a genie's bottle.
Tried to spirit something
of Mother from the rings
and into me.

A deep yearning had settled.
I needed Annie.
My dear, dear Annie,
who had disappeared
like a broken spell when
I spoke her name to Jeffrey.

PHOTOGRAPHIC EVIDENCE I

I took my camera everywhere
and photographed what I saw.

I collected images of feathers
and half-eaten plums,

of bones and skulls, of maggots
eating the inside of a blackbird,

of a decomposing kangaroo
lying on the side of the road,

its mouth ajar as if in surprise,
eyes dull and dry in death.

Its stomach had a wound
where large birds had been feasting.

There was a stain around the body
like a dark shadow.

Its left foot was severed, but for
a sliver of fur.

I took Father's small knife
from my pocket and sliced it free.

Photographed the paw,
the black claws.

Then wrapped it up
took it home.

MOTHER MEMORY VI

Mother is leaning over my bed.
She has woken me gently
from a shallow sleep.

Her face is shadowy
in the dim room.
I inhale her perfume.

Her hair tickles my face.
I run a strand along my cheek,
as soft as a feather.

Be good for your father,
she whispers.
Her breath is fresh and sweet,
as if she has just eaten
fruit salad and honey.

Be good while I am gone.
She unwraps her hair from my fingers,
kisses my hand and cheek,
offers a sad smile
and glides away.

Gone.

GOLDEN BANDS I

The next day I slipped the rings
from my fingers,
placed them on Father's desk.

He picked them up,
turned them over and over.

I found them in a pocket
in Mother's long black coat
in this folded envelope.

Father slipped them on
his ring finger
up to knuckle—
as far as they would go.

I thought they were lost,
gone forever.
I must have put them in the coat.
I don't remember.

His words were as heavy
as an anchor thrown to sea.

Your mother took the rings
from her swollen fingers
before the birth.

The golden bands shone;
the diamonds glittered.

She asked the nurse
to keep them safe
until I arrived.

We never saw her again.

He took a long, long breath.

Not alive.

GOLDEN BANDS II

Were you happy together?
Did you love her?
I wanted to know.

Yes, I loved her very much.
Yes, we were happy. Once. Often.

But not always. Not in the photographs.
Or in my memories.

Not when Annie died.
We did not cope, I suppose.

But even before—in the photos.
You both look sad.

The war years took their toll.
My father, your grandfather, died.

Your mother and grandmother
had to fend for themselves—

farm the land,
feed themselves.

Your mother was weak from hunger,
weak from the work,

even after the war
when Annie was born.

And then you arrived,
and then the other baby,

carried to term and lost.
Lost.

Both of them gone…

THE SADNESS LINGERED

Your mother was fragile—
we lost many relatives
through the war.

We suffered
the indignity of being imprisoned
by our adopted country.

Family and friends
died in the war.
Some at the hands of the Nazis.

Your mother had Jewish relatives
and friends who disappeared.
People she loved.

Those years after the war
were not easy.
The sadness lingered,

but nothing compared
to the loss
of our dear, dear Annie.

She was such a joy.
She was the sunshine
we longed for.

And then she was gone.

WHAT OF MOTHER?

Father cleared his throat.
The baby was stillborn…
He looked out the window.

I nodded, said: *Yes, yes.*
I wanted more.
I wanted it all.

He had skirted
and sidestepped this
too many times.

We never spoke of death.
We never spoke of Mother.
We never spoke of Annie.

Your mother was not strong;
she had suffered for years—
since the war.

She died during the birth,
of the birth.

They said it was
a blood infection,

but I think she died
of a broken heart.

DYING MANY DEATHS

I thought back to Father's words:
She died of a broken heart.

And to Annie's words:
*Jill fell down and
broke her crown and Jack
came tumbling after.*

Father tumbled
when Mother died.

We all died
when Annie died.

We all died, again,
when Mother died.

Death haunted us all
in our own ways.

Annie had said: *It is only death.
It is not the end!*

*The dead are gone—
not forgotten.*

*We all die.
It's a part of life.*

MOSAIC MEMORIES

After our talk
I thought about
my memories of Mother,
those strange fragments
that haunted
and confused.

But now
with Father's words
those memories
seemed less disjointed
more whole, like
mosaic tiles.

HUNTING I

Jeffrey was a good friend,
a good distraction,
who kept my mind from wandering
to Annie and Mother.
We met after school,
went hunting.

He was a good tracker.
He could find
all sorts of things
to which my eyes and ears
were blind.

We found birds and lizards
and berries and grubs.
He pointed to the tracks
of kangaroos and echidnas
in the scrub.

I took photos of birds
and mammals and reptiles, and
of Jeffrey's beautiful smile.

HUNTING II

One day we crouched
watching a mob of kangaroos.
So rare to see them
so close to the suburbs.
So rare for us
to be so close.

When I turned to speak
I saw Jeffrey's long-lashed
chocolate eyes and his wide smile.
I reached out, touched his hand,
leaned in,
and we fell into
a soft, slow kiss.

JEWELS I

The first storm after the summer
drenched.
The wide cracks in the earth
drank the cool clear rainwater.

Jeffery and I were out walking
the paddocks that skirt the town
when thunder clouds rolled in
and forks of lightning split the sky.

We sheltered under an ancient gum
by the creek, and listened
to the trickle of water, to the rain and
thunder and shriek of birds.

Jeffrey carefully lifted some bark
and uncovered a tiny skeleton,
curled in a foetal position
clinging to its long slender tail.

Is it a mouse? I asked.
He shook his head. *Baby possum.*
The beautiful precision—
complete, not one piece missing.

Its tiny bones: the fragile ribs,
long-fingered hands and toes.
Its mouth, slightly ajar,
with tiny teeth.

It was as beautiful as a jewel,
as beautiful as Jeffrey's eyes.
It reminded me of the dying
possum near Oma's farm.

JEWELS II

It rained for a week,
keeping me inside watching
the rain-streaked windows
and the garden changing colour
from a weary grey
to a bright green.

The glory vine glowed
with iridescence—
yellows, oranges and deep reds.

I had time to sift and
sort my photos.
To study their composition,
the nuances of tone
and subject—
the newly dead,
the decomposing,
the skeletal.

PHOTOGRAPHIC EVIDENCE II

Aunt Hilda was not pleased.
I could hear her voice
through the thick walls.

I opened the bedroom door,
listened to her and Father
through the crack.

She is wearing the fox to school.
She is drawing pictures of the dead.
She is taking photographs of death.

Her workbooks are full of pictures
of tombstones and graveyards.
She is writing poems about dying.

Her teachers are concerned.
Wolfgang, this is not healthy!
This is serious!

Her room has that smell again.
The smell of death and decay.

Wolfgang, she is not well.
When will you see?
You must stop this.

I crept up the hall, avoiding
the creaky floorboard, peeked through
the gap in the sliding door.

Father flicked through
my treasured photographs,
his frown deep.

What shall we do, Wolfgang?
Confiscate the camera?

REBELLION

I burst in, roared:
You will not take my camera!
You are not my mother!

Lottie! That is enough,
Father's voice boomed.
Show some respect!

After all your aunt has done
for you, for us!

Young Lady, out now!
Go to your room.

BAD DREAMS

My eyes were gritty
from tears and anger.

My body heavy
with the dead weight of grief.

For hours Aunt Hilda and Father
talked and talked.

Their words indecipherable
through the walls.

I hovered over sleep,
drifting, finally,
into bad dreams.

BONES AND BEAKS AND FEATHERS

Before leaving for school
I gathered
the other photographs—
the ones Father developed,
the ones Aunt Hilda had not seen—
that I'd kept
in my bedside drawer.

I took the fragile skeleton
of the baby possum,
the skulls of birds,
the flight and tail feathers
of brown hawks
and parrots and lorikeets
and the decaying paw
of the kangaroo.

I carried them to the shed,
hid them
in Father's cupboard,
away from Aunt Hilda's
prying eyes.

BREAKFAST

At breakfast Aunt Hilda sat opposite
and said in a quiet, calm voice:

Your Father and I talked.
He said he is going to fix this.
He told me he will end it
once and for all.

She reached out,
touched my hand.

Lottie, my dear,
I know you think I am harsh
but I just want to be a good aunt.
I want what is best for you.
One day you will see.

All day at school
Aunt Hilda's words
reverberated
along with Annie's:

It's only death.
It's not the end.
We all die.

They pinged through my head,
an unwanted refrain.

I looked for Annie, but
she was nowhere.

CARTWHEELS II

A bank of grey clouds
skimmed the chalky-blue sky.

The sun was soft, the wind, sharp,
cutting through my thin T-shirt.

Russet-coloured leaf litter
skittered and somersaulted

and a claw-shaped leaf
cartwheeled in front of me.

The ground was dry again
and cracked from the summer heat.

Brittle leaves, twigs and bark
crunched under my feet.

Up ahead a small group of magpies
speared the ground.

They are not a small group,
Annie's voice sang in my head.

*They are a tittering, a tiding, a char,
a congregation, or a murder.*

Their warbling song normally
filled me with cheer,

but today it was a song of sadness,
a mourning song.

THE BROKEN, THE BATTERED, THE DEAD

After school I went to my room,
shut the door, lay on my bed.
But the door flew open.

I found your ghoulish stash
hidden in the shed. The box full of
the broken, the battered, the dead.

Where are they?
What have you done?
Tears were already falling.

They are confiscated.
I have done you a favour.
It is time to move on.
Your father agrees.

Aunt Hilda shut the door firmly.
I rolled on my side,
curled into foetal position
like the precious baby possum.

FOETAL

I did not move,
I would not eat,
I could not move,
I could not eat.

Aunt Hilda and Father's voices
rose and fell in a distant place.

Their faces, their brows
crinkled with concern,
hovered above,
drifted in and out of focus.

I wanted my baby possum.
I wanted my beautiful
taxidermied bird.

I wanted my creatures,
I wanted my treasures,
I wanted my mother.

I wanted my Annie.

ANNIE III

She came in a dream,
curled her
beautiful white body
around me.

Her sunshiny hair
tickled my cheek.

We lay together
for a long time—
and then she said:

All will be well,
you will see.
Tomorrow, rise early.
Talk to Father.
Tell him
how you feel.

SUNRISE

I walked down the hall
to Father's room,
sat on the end of his bed.
He woke with surprise.
Lottie. Are you all right?

Yes, Father.
I need to tell you that I am not
what you and Aunt Hilda think I am.
I do not go around killing.
I would never do that.

I love animals. I would never harm them.
It is not macabre or ghoulish
to hold on, to resurrect,
to re-imagine, to re-create.

It is a way of honouring beauty.
It is a way to hold onto life.

I am a girl, but I am not
Aunt Hilda's girl,
and I am not like her.

Father reached out
and tucked a strand of hair
behind my ear,
just like Mother or Oma
would have done.

Lottie, your aunt loves you.
She is worried and
she means well.

She wants what is best
for you.

We both do.

RETURNING TO THE WORLD

I returned to the world,
reinhabited my body,
to a degree.
It felt unfamiliar,
as if it had grown
since my retreat,
my inward turn.

The long walk to school
felt miraculous,
the world appeared hyperreal,
the colours brighter,
the sky higher,
the trees, the grass, the leaves
sharp-edged,
more defined.

And I had a sense
of drifting above myself
just out of reach.

COLD GREY STREETS

Jeffrey smiled his slow smile
from across the quadrangle
and sauntered towards me.

He did not ask where I had been.
We just fell into step,
walked to class.

All day I drifted in and out
of my body,
watched myself from afar.

Every now and then
thoughts of my spoiled treasures
slipped into my mind.

Heaviness descended,
filling my legs with lead,
my eyes with salty tears.

On the way home I dragged
my weary feet
along cold grey streets
under a thick blanket of cloud.

I meandered across paddocks,
under canopies of trees,
crunching over deep layers
of mouldering leaves,

trying to conjure Annie
trying to re-enter
that long-ago dream.

ANSWERS

And then, as if in reply,
the sun burst through
a glorious hole in the clouds
sending shafts of light
onto a bony-shape
beneath the leafy litter
at my feet.

I bent down, uncovered
smooth white bone
and the delicate skull
of a small cat.

Six tiny incisors,
two perfectly sharpened eye teeth,
maxilla and molars—
all pristine,
glinting in the sudden sunshine.

A fissure from the nose cavity
to the base of the skull
divided the hemispheres
left and right—
right and wrong?

It revived me,
this bony message—
this feline find.
Such perfect precision,
so light, so white,
so wild, so right.

There it was,
out of nowhere
into my hands,
as if it contained the answer
to everything.

RECONSTRUCTING

I combed through leaves
and damp soil
uncovering bone after bone:
clavicle, scapula,
vertebra, pelvis,
fibula, femur,
metatarsal,
phalange.

I imagined myself
in an ancient land,

sifting through soil and sand
on an archaeological dig.

Each bony find brought pleasure,
a tingling delight, and

as I reconstructed
this treasure, this gift,
these skeletal remains,

I felt my own bones lighten.

BONES

I hid away in my room,
made a shoebox nest
for my new treasures,
but not for the skull.

I wanted it on display,
upfront, central,
its presence alive,
powerful.

I put the skull
on my bedside chest
like an ancient talisman
to bring me luck
and keep me buoyant.

It filled the air with the energy
of ancient Egypt
and the cat goddess, Bastet.

In those delicate
bones and teeth
were the elements
and minerals
of stars and stardust
and all of the people
I ever loved.

STILL LIFE WITH SKULL

I heard Aunt Hilda's voice
hazy and distant
calling me to dinner.

But it barely penetrated
my focus,
enthralled as I was
with my feline treasure.

Under the yellow light
of my bedside lamp
the cat skull glowed warmly,
painterly,
as if a master artist
had created it
stroke by oily stroke.

I gathered a few objects:
a book, a scarf, a speckled egg,
placed them with the skull—
artfully arranged.

I examined my still life
through the lens of my camera,
opened the aperture wide,
set a long exposure,
focused, steadied and,
at the slow click of the shutter,
the bedroom door opened.

Aunt Hilda stood in the doorway,
eyes wide and white
at the sight of that skull
illuminated in golden light.

SILENCE II

Aunt Hilda said nothing
at dinner
to Father or me
about the skull.

We all sat quietly for a while,
till Father said:

It is good to have you back, Lottie.
We missed you at the table.

Didn't we, Hilda?

Yes, Lottie. It is good
that you are feeling better.

We were worried.

And then we returned
to silence.

POWER

School was torturous—
a long, slow walk
through fog.

I missed Annie;
I could not cling
to Jeffrey all day.

I wandered through the hours
from class to class
mostly alone.

All week I wandered.
All week I wondered
when the skull would be removed.

But it stayed.
Each day there it was,
unmoved, untouched,

exuding its fierce power,
though my own power
eluded me.

FELINE

One day I arrived home
feeling low, bereft,
expecting the skull
to be confiscated, gone, forever lost.

I walked into the house,
down the gloomy hall
into my room to see
the skull, still there,

on the bedside chest
undisturbed.
Still radiating
beauty and power, but—

there on my bed
was a cardboard box
that made a sound—a scratch,
a muffled squeak.

I peered inside
and in a nest of fine straw
was a black furry ball
with piercing yellow eyes.

AUNT HILDA'S REMEDY

The door creaked behind me
as I picked up
this living, breathing creature.

Lottie, do you like her?

Yes! Yes, I do!

I cupped the tiny
almost-weightless body
in my hands.

Held her to my cheek,
felt her soft fur,
her purr, her warmth.

Then Aunt Hilda gathered me
into her fleshy arms
and held me tight.

This is what you need,
my dear Lottie.
Life, not death. Life.

She will be a good friend.
You will see.

CLEOPATRA

I called my kitten Cleo,
short for Cleopatra,
after the Egyptian queen.

I adored the mummified cats
I had seen in books,
dressed in straitjacket bandages,
wrapped up, swaddled tightly
like newborn babies.

I once saw a picture
of a mummified cat, unwrapped.
Its face was set
in an infinite scream.

The Egyptians idolised
domestic cats, though
Bastet the cat goddess
was a warrior lioness.

My mini lioness, Cleo,
was a furry enchantress.
When I played with her
everything else
melted away.

BLACK

She was a piece of midnight,
as dark as the unlit corners
of a shadowy room.

Her paws were pins,
her teeth, needles,
her ears, radars,
her eyes, golden stones.

At night she came alive,
her pupils opened wide
into black moons.

She was a curl of cat
sleeping in the shape of
a comma—
a pause of pleasure.

She slept on my lap
or at the end of my bed
or by my pillowed head.

And if I could not find her
I'd need only look
for Aunt Hilda, who
gave her milky treats,

whispered into her furry ears
and smiled and purred
as if *she* were the cat
being loved.

COUNSELLING

During dinner Father opened his letters,
eyebrows raised in interest.

Lottie, this is from your school.
You will have a career counsellor
attending soon.

You need to think about your future,
about what you'd like to do.

Perhaps you would like to go
to teachers' college or university.

Yes! A teacher, Aunt Hilda agreed.
Or you might like to be a nurse.

No! I know exactly what I want to do.
I want to work at the museum.
I want to study taxidermy.

Aunt Hilda stopped eating,
her loaded fork paused mid-air.

Oh, Charlotte! No, not that, please.
Her voice was tinged with despair.

Nursing is respectable, fitting.
Nursing would be perfect.

Look how kind and caring you are
with your little kitten.

LAYING OUT THE BONES

That night I sat in my room
with Aunt Hilda's words
running through my skull.

I did not want to teach.
I did not want to nurse.
I knew what I wanted to do.

I could hear the rumblings
of debate rolling down the hall.

To distract myself I lay out the bones
of my feline find, while Cleo watched,

guarding, her golden eyes intense,
her tail twitching, her body sprung.

Finding the shape of the cat
was like drawing with bones.

I puzzled over my skeletal jigsaw
as if reconstructing a dinosaur.

The joy of re-creating
tingled through my body—

reconfirmed
what I already knew.

EMPTY TOMBS

I had not visited Mother's room
for a long time,
not since Father spoke of her,
not since we talked about her rings.

The room—cold, as chilly as a morgue—
was clean and clinical,
the surfaces bare
of Mother and her possessions.

I sat on her bed, alone,
feeling hollow,
thinking of all her beautiful things
out in the shed.

It was time to fill the emptiness
to warm the heart
of this grief-stricken place.
Time to put things right.

RESURRECTING MOTHER

I brought her back
from the dead,
from the dark
of the shed.

Brought her back
to life, to live
inside.

I filled her drawers
and wardrobe
with her clothes.

Her trinkets
and perfume,
her brush and comb.

Little by little, I restored,
replaced, resurrected and
reinstated her
where she belonged.

THE DEAD OF NIGHT

A shaft of light woke me
in the dead of night.

When I crept to my door,
peered into the hall,

I saw Father in the gloom,
hands in pockets,

at the doorway
of Mother's room.

His sad face
stared

at the restoration,
the revival of her tomb.

From the way he stood, staring,
I knew he approved.

FATHER'S REMEDY II

Father carried a package
under his arm.

He had a solemn look
on his face.

I unwrapped the brown paper
and found a book.

Inside the book
there were photographs
of animals
in various stages of repair.

All of them dead.
All of them
exquisitely remade.

THE FINAL WORD

Later that evening
I heard her shrill voice:
This is wrong, Wolfgang!
I cannot stand by and watch.
Charlotte is a girl! A girl!

If she were a boy it might not be
so strange, but
who will marry a girl, a woman
who stuffs the hides of animals?

Father replied in his no-nonsense tone:
This is the way it will be.
Her interest is unusual
but not unhealthy—
not for a scientist.

I know you love Lottie.
You have cared for her
just like a mother,
but she must be
who she needs to be.

It might be just curiosity.
It might be just a phase,
but if it is not
then we will channel it properly.

And she is not cruel or unkind.
Hilda, you saw it yourself,
how much she dotes
on her little kitten.

THE SMELL OF DEATH

The next day we visited
the museum.
Father had arranged a time
to see the taxidermist.

My stomach was queasy
when we arrived—
I was so nervous,
excited.

The smell of death
hung in the air
as we entered
the studio.

The taxidermist
showed me freezers full
of animals
waiting to be
re-created.

THE TAXIDERMIST I

The taxidermist asked about my interests
as he set up his tools
on a glinting stainless-steel bench.

He told me that he had
three dogs two cats,
four children and a wife.
He said he had a normal life.

He told me his father
was also a taxidermist,
that he never wanted
to do anything else.

If you are keen, I will help you
skin and mount a hopping mouse.

Perhaps, one day you will join me
at the museum.

THE TAXIDERMIST II

The taxidermist was interested
to hear of my past efforts,
and saddened but not
surprised to hear of Aunt Hilda.

She means well, I'm sure.
It is hard for people to grasp
this love.

Most people come to the museum
and look in awe
at the taxidermy animals.

They do not think about the process,
about the smell or the mess,
or the care taken,

or about the determination,
the anatomical knowledge
and the love in the work.

They will not even register
the death. But we do.

We see it, and we feel it,

and this is how we honour it.

THE TAXIDERMIST III

Father approved
of my first taxidermy piece.
He held it up, studied it
for a very long time.

It's a fawn hopping mouse, I said.
Notomys cervinus, *from*
the Lake Eyre Basin.

A gregarious mouse that feeds
at night on seeds and insects
and does not need to drink water.

It is perfect, Father said.
You are a true scientist
and a talented artist.

Father's words lifted me,
filled me to the brim.

This is what I want to be.
Father, I am certain
I want to work at the museum.

I want to be a taxidermist.
I feel it in my heart.
I will study very hard.

I will do everything I can
to make this transcendent art.

FUNERAL BIRDS II

We drove to Oma's
on the weekend
for Opa's birthday,
as we do every year.

When we stood at the foot
of Opa's grave, Annie's words
skipped through my head.
We all die, we all die.

And for a moment I felt
her presence
and optimism lift me,
as if she were really there.

And then as if to give me a sign
there in the distant sky
like slender darts
were two black cockatoos.

The Funeral Birds—*Wylah,*
Wy-lah, Wy-lah.
They floated over us
crying their mournful cry.

Oma wept and nodded her head,
muttering German words
and prayers,
as if agreeing with the birds.

Soon, I realised, she and Opa
would both be buried here.
She would join him
in this graveyard.

GROUNDED

Father put his arm around
Oma's thin shoulders, briefly,

while I drifted over
to Mother and Annie.

I stared
at their headstones

with a deep ache
in my chest,

wishing I could
resurrect them.

Aunt Hilda joined me,
planted her solid feet next to mine.

We stood in silence
side-by-side.

I noticed how grounded
her feet appeared—

how firm,
how resolute,

as I stared at her brown shoes
and listened to her soft wheezy breath.

She slid an arm around my shoulder,
squeezed and said:

I miss them too, dear Lottie.
I miss them every day.

My eyes burned with tears,
my focus blurred,

her shoes became fuzzy,
dissolved into the earth.

Aunt Hilda pulled me closer
and I wept on her shoulder.

ENDINGS

Endings can be a form
of death.

Jeffrey was leaving
with his foster family,

moving to another suburb
in another town.

Jeffrey, my only friend,
the love of my short life,

would soon be gone
and the ache

was softened only
by the promise of letters,

the promise
that we'd always be friends.

Jeffrey did not approve
of taxidermy

but I gave him
the little hopping mouse.
He studied it quietly
and smiled when I said:

It was made with love
and carries
a small piece of my heart.

THE ART OF TAXIDERMY

I practised my art,
brought home the dead,
worked meticulously
and methodically.

I skinned and stuffed and mounted
mice and rats and birds and
lizards—any critters
I could find.

I remade them, modelled them,
wired and posed them until
they appeared alive,
about to leap or hop or fly.

In my makeshift laboratory
when focused on my work,
I felt close to Mother and
dear, dear Annie.

It dulled the bone-heavy
ache of grief—

the revitalisation of life,
the bringing back
from the edge
of decay.

The revival and
re-creation of something
that has expired
is an honour
and a gift.

ACKNOWLEDGMENTS

First, thanks to everyone at Text Publishing for being so supportive and enthusiastic. Special thanks to my wonderful editor, Jane Pearson, for her insightful feedback and suggestions.

This novel may never have been written if it were not for the generous funding of an Arts SA project grant to complete the first draft. Huge thanks to Jude Aquilina and Louise Nicholas for taking the time to write letters of support for the project.

In addition, I'd like to thank all the writers in my life—it's great to be a part of such a vibrant, passionate community of creative people. Special thanks to Gay Lynch, Danielle Clode and Doug Stevenson, who read early drafts of the manuscript and provided valuable feedback; to my dear friend, Helen Lindstrom, for her unflinching support; to Ray Clift for his friendship; and to the late Ken Vincent, who would have loved this project.

Thank you Tony and Wendy Fawcus for the month-long stay at Brooklands Heritage B&B in Port Elliot, where I wrote and revised many scenes. To Rosemary

Gower of the Loveday Internment Camp Museum for information about the camp, the internees, and the Barmera Cemetery. To Marianna Datsenko for reading the manuscript and assisting with the German phrases and pronunciations. And finally, thank you always to my wonderful family—Mum and Dad, and Matt and Jess for their unconditional support, patience, love and encouragement; to my brothers, David, for writerly conversations, and Rob, for bushwalks and bird watching; and to Gary for his ongoing presence, enthusiasm and belief in this project and all the others.